FIGHTING FOR THE FORBIDDEN

TRACY LORRAINE

Copyright © 2019 by Tracy Lorraine

All rights reserved.

No part of this book may be reproduced in any form or by any electronic or mechanical means, including information storage and retrieval systems, without written permission from the author, except for the use of brief quotations in a book review.

Edited by Pinpoint Editing

Proofread by Andie M. Long

Photography by James Critchley

Model George RJ

Cover design and formatting by Dandelion Cover Designs

Andy and Amelia

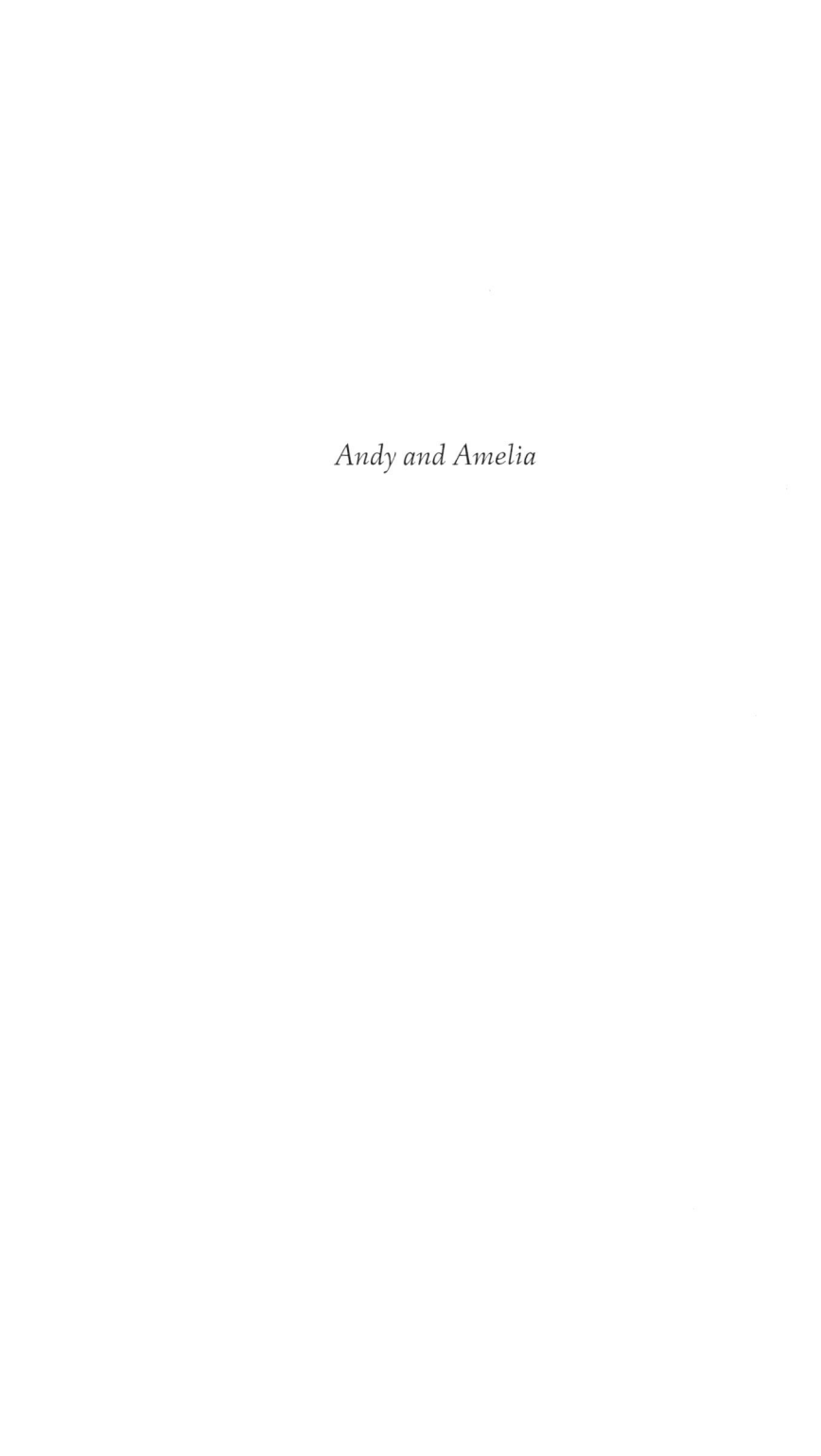

PROLOGUE

Lauren

THE SECOND THE door slams shut, I turn into Joe's chest. Squeezing my eyes shut, I fight my need to break down, but the devastation running through my body is too strong.

I just did the one thing I never thought I'd be strong enough to do.

I sent the only man I've ever loved away.

Joe's strong arms wrap around my body and he whispers 'everything's okay' in my ear. I don't believe a word of it. How can anything be okay when it hurts this fucking much?

With my heart in pieces, I give myself over to my tears. I suck in deep lungfuls of air as I sob into the hot skin of his chest.

His hands softly rub my back, but it does nothing to soothe the pain. Nothing in the world can make what I just did any better.

The hurt in Ben's eyes as he looked at the two of us is going to be forever in my mind. I'd always hoped that I'd get the chance to do to him what he did to me the day he left. I hoped in some fucked up way that it would make it all right, but the crack in my heart that I've been living with for the past six years is now bigger than ever.

I'd convinced myself that he obviously didn't love me back then; that in the long run, him walking away was the best thing that could have happened. I'd fallen head over heels so fast that the longer it lasted, the more it was going to hurt when it ended.

But the man I just sent away isn't one who doesn't care. He's a man who loves me just as much now as he did back then. His feelings were written all over his face; they have been since the day he walked back into the office like no time had passed.

Everything I thought I knew has been smashed to pieces over the last couple of days, and right now, I don't know which way is fucking up.

It's not until Joe's warmth leaves me that I realise he's moved us to the sofa.

"You did the right thing there, sweets," he says, wrapping his hand around the back of my head and kissing my forehead. He rests his lips there for a few seconds, and I'm reminded of everything this man has given me.

He appeared in my life just at the right time. If it weren't for him, I've no idea how I'd have got my life back on track after Ben left. Somehow he managed to pick me up and point me in the right direction, something everyone else around me failed to achieve.

Fate brought us together, and I'll forever be grateful that he turned up looking for a job when he did. He's been my rock this week. He's done every single thing I've asked of him, which is why he's the one drying my tears right now. My body trembles once again as memories from only moments ago at our door hit me.

My head might tell me that it was the right thing to do, but it seems my heart has another opinion.

CHAPTER ONE

Ben

"BEN?" Mum calls, following my footsteps from only seconds ago. "Ben, what the hell are you..." She trails off when she takes in the scene in front of her. "No. No, you're not going." Reaching out, she snatches my bag from the bed and frantically turns it over so she can shake out everything I'd just shoved inside. She doesn't stop until the bag's completely empty.

Her face twists with emotion and panic. "You're not doing this. You're not leaving."

"It's over."

"No, it's not. It's just the beginning. Please, Ben. Please." Her voice cracks, and the sound is like another knife to my heart.

All my life, I've only ever wanted to protect the two women I love, but at every turn, the only thing I seem to do is hurt them.

"It's best for everyone if I just leave. I'm causing too much pain."

She watches as I throw all the clothes I have back into my small holdall. She's deep in thought, presumably trying to come up with a way to make me stay, but I think we both know she's not going to win this fight.

"You're not. I love having you back. It's been an emotional week. We all just need a little time to find a new rhythm and get back to some kind of normal. Everything will be fine."

"I'm so fed up of everyone saying that. How is everything going to be okay, Mum? Huh? The business is one bad job away from going under. This place...well," I throw my arms out in defeat. "And Lauren. She's moved on. She doesn't want me."

"She's scared, Ben."

"She didn't look that scared in *his* arms."

Mum opens her mouth to say something but

changes her mind at the last minute. "Put yourself in her shoes. Just give her time."

"Fuck time," I spit. "It's been *six years*. It's now or never."

"You don't mean that."

"Don't I?"

"This is my fault," she mutters, spinning on the spot and pulling her hair back from her face. Stopping what I'm doing, I stare at her, waiting for her to say more. When her eyes find mine again, guilt oozes from them.

"What did you do?"

"I..." She hesitates and my pulse picks up speed. "You need to remember that I'm trying to support both of you here."

"What. Did. You. Do?" I spit, my frustration building with her bullshit stalling tactics.

"I warned Lauren that you were on your way."

The fear on Lauren's face when she first opened the door earlier fills my mind; her hesitance to say or do anything as I stared back at her.

"*You* set that up? *You* put me through that?" I roar, not really believing what I'm hearing. "I had to stand there and watch him with his hands all over her because of *you*? Whose side exactly are you on here?"

"I'm not on anyone's side, Ben."

"Bullshit. I'm your son. You're meant to be helping *me*." I know I'm being irrational, but the image of them barely dressed at their front door is burned into my eyes.

"I am, I am. But Lauren's—"

"Lauren's what? More important?"

"No, no. She's like a daughter to me, Ben. Over the past six years we've become close. I don't want to see her hurt either."

"So it's okay for *me* to be the one hurt? This is fucking bullshit. I knew coming back here was a bad idea. I'm done." Storming past Mum, I knock into her shoulder and she stumbles back into the door.

"Ben, please," she wails. "You can't leave. What about your stuff?"

"I left with nothing once before. I can do it again."

The sound of her cries hardly filters through the anger racing around my body as I storm from the house and jump in my car.

The roar of the engine does little to settle me, but the knowledge that I'm escaping helps a little. Running is probably the coward's way out, but right now I don't really give a fuck.

I drive around the city for the longest time, taking

in the sights I grew up with as my anger slowly starts to simmer down. I intend on this being the last time I'm here for the foreseeable future. Once I've had my fill, I head towards the motorway that will take me home.

The ringing of my phone cuts through the silence in the car.

Erica's name flashes on the dashboard. I want to ignore it, but at the last minute my thumb hits the accept button.

"Ben, are you there?" she asks after a few seconds of silence.

"Yeah."

"Is everything okay? You sound weird."

"I'm leaving."

"You're what?" she shouts, the volume making me jump and swerve the car. "You can't leave. What's happened?"

Looking up, I spot a sign for a place I haven't been in a really, really long time. "Hang on, I'm just pulling over."

Bringing the car to a stop in the almost deserted car park, I rest my head back.

"It's over, Erica. I was stupid to think I could turn up here and everything would just fall into place. I'm not needed here anymore."

"Stop talking shit, of course you're needed. *I* need you. I know I don't deserve it after what I did, but I need your help fixing everything I've done wrong. Your mum needs you. You've no idea how hard it's been for her without you. And she might not show it, but Lauren needs you. She—"

"She's got him. She said it herself, she's moved on."

"Do you truly believe that, Ben?"

After tonight, I want to say yes, but then I think about the small amount of time we've spend together over the last few days. The look in her eyes as she gazed up at me, the gentleness of her touch, her genuine smile when I caught her off guard. "I don't know," I admit quietly.

"I never thought you were the kind of guy who'd run the moment things got hard. I always thought you'd fight for what you really wanted, especially now you've got this second chance."

My lips press into a thin line as her words hit exactly where she intended.

"You'll regret leaving like this, and you know it."

"I...I need to go." I force the words out through the lump in my throat and hang up. She's right; I would regret not knowing what could have been, but does that mean I've got the strength to stay and fight this out?

With my eyes tightly shut, I blow a long stream of air past my lips. Everything that's happened in the last few days plays out like a movie in my mind. The arguments, the sorrow, the desire, the despair. Lauren's face as she asked me to just lie with her the other night when she was so lost. Mum's haunted eyes when she learnt the truth about her late husband. Can I walk away right now knowing how much they're both hurting? Even if I caused some of it?

My thoughts are warring in my head as I push the door open and head out into the late summer evening. The sun's just starting to set, casting everything in a soft orange glow. It almost makes this place look inviting.

I pass a couple of other people on the way, but no one pays me any attention, all too consumed by their own grief.

I've only been here once before, but that doesn't mean I don't know exactly where he is. I might have just been a kid, but every second of that devastating day is etched into my mind.

Mum tried convincing me to come here in the months after we lost him, but I always refused, not really understanding how standing and staring at a headstone could possibly help me.

As I come to stand in front of the place we laid my dad to rest twelve years ago, the same emptiness engulfs me like the first time I was standing in this exact place. I don't think I'll ever really come to terms with losing him the way I did.

Dad was my best friend, my hero, my idol. He was there playing football with me in the back garden one day, and then the next I was forced to say my final goodbye to him.

I guess I shouldn't be surprised to find a bunch of fresh flowers placed next to his headstone. I knew Mum used to come here on a weekly basis, but I kind of assumed that had stopped after marrying Nick. I guess I was wrong. It's not unusual these days.

Sitting myself on the patch of grass in front of the stone, I think back over my memories with Dad. All of them are happy. I can't help but wonder how my life might be different right now if he hadn't passed so early.

I probably wouldn't have met Lauren.

My breath catches as the thought really hits me. Lauren has been by far the best thing that ever happened to me. Our story might be full of pain and heartache, but still, she gave me something that I've not found anywhere else. She showed me what love really is and why it's worth risking everything for.

My fists clench as what I was about to walk away from really hits me. If I leave now, all of our past is for nothing. If I walk away now, then it's my choice. *I'm* the one putting the final nail in the coffin where our relationship is concerned. What we had all those years ago is worth more than me walking away.

Standing, a new lease of determination runs through me.

I've dealt with worse than this.

I've perfected the skill of pulling on a mask to get through the hard times, and if I have to revert to old tactics as I wait Lauren out, then I will.

I can put Ben and all his feelings back inside the box he's been shoved in for the past six years.

It's time for London to meet BJ.

CHAPTER TWO

Lauren

"SEE, I told you this was a good idea," Joe says as we walk toward the entrance of Sixty4, our go-to bar a couple of streets away.

Once my tears started to dry up, Joe announced that we were going out for cocktails. To say I wasn't really in the mood was an understatement, but he was insistent that I would feel better for it.

I hate to admit it, but with a ton of concealer around my eyes, my favourite dress and my cute peep-toe heels, I do feel just a little bit better.

Someone waving from just inside the door

catches my eye, and my face splits into a wide smile when I find Danni, my best friend, waiting for me.

"I thought you had loads of uni work to do?" I say, throwing my arms around her shoulders.

"I do, but Joe said you needed to get out of the house. Is everything okay?"

Joe pipes up before I get a chance. I'm grateful because I don't really want to think about what happened tonight, let alone talk about it. "Ben's just being a little overbearing."

The image of him standing at our front door earlier has my eyes stinging, but thankfully no tears come. I think I've probably run out.

"What are we waiting for then? Let's get a drink down us."

"Thank you," I whisper, terrified of breaking down while surrounded by strangers.

"It's two-for-one night." With my arms linked with my friends, they drag me towards the bar and order our first drinks.

The alcohol and the sweetness of the fruit juice definitely does help to cheer me up a little, but at no point does the image of his devastated face leave me. I swear it's going to be there forever, always making me wonder if I made the worst decision of my life by sending him away.

"Earth to Lauren," Joe sings, waving a fresh vodka martini in front of me.

"Sorry," I mutter. I hate the sympathetic eyes I get from both of them, but I've no idea how to attempt to convince them that I'm fine.

"So, any guys taking your fancy?" I ask Danni, trying to take the heat off me and my disastrous love life.

She glances around briefly before turning back and shaking her head. "Is your dry spell that bad?" Joe asks before Danni launches into explaining the handful of disastrous dates she's been on recently. I totally zone out, and it's not until my phone starts vibrating in my bag that I come back to myself.

"If that's him, don't answer," Joe warns when he sees me pull my phone out.

"It's not. I'm sorry," I say, excusing myself when I see Jenny's name on the screen. I know I should probably ignore her for the night as well, but I can't. She seems to be coping with everything better now that Ben's here, but I still worry about her.

"Hello."

"Hello. Lauren? Are you there? Hello?" I walk to the bar entrance as fast as I can so she can hear me over the commotion behind me.

"Yeah, I'm here. Sorry, I'm out with friends."

"Oh...uh...sorry, I'll leave you, then."

The sadness in her tone has me encouraging her to talk. "No, it's fine. What's up?"

"It's...Ben."

All the air rushes from my lungs. Of course it bloody is.

"What about him?"

"I told him that I'd warned you he was coming. He was furious."

"Right?"

"He left. I think he's really gone this time, and it's all m-my f-fault," she sobs.

I bite back the response that's on the tip of my tongue, because the guilt I feel for being responsible fills me.

"I can't lose him again, Lauren. I can't. He's all I've got." Her sobs get louder, and the words are out of my mouth before I've really considered the consequences.

"I'll find him."

Jenny might not be my mum, but living in her house for the past six years meant that we'd bonded and I'd do almost anything to ensure that she's happy. It's more than my dad did for her in the years they were together.

"You will?"

"I'll do my best."

Hanging up, I glance back into the bar at Danni and Joe, who are laughing away like they've not got a care in the world. It would probably make my life easier if I asked for their help, but I've got a pretty good idea what their opinion on all of this would be. They both agree that I need to stay as far away from Ben as I can. Most of the time I agree with them—well, my head does. But this isn't about me. This is about Jenny. She's already been through more pain and heartache than most people should have to deal with in their lifetime.

Squaring my shoulders, I look back one last time before walking away from the bar and going in search of a taxi. Once I'm settled, I send a quick text to Joe and Danni to explain my disappearance before putting my phone back in my bag and staring out the window.

When the taxi pulls into the car park, I'm convinced that his car is going to be parked in the far corner. It's his favourite place; the place he comes when he needs some peace and to get away from the world.

But it's empty.

Not knowing what my next move will be, I ask the driver to pull up and wait. I get out and the low evening sun immediately warms my skin. Walking to the edge of the gravel, I look out at the city beyond. So much has happened between us in this deserted car park. It makes me feel closer to him just by being here. I've no idea how he ever found this place, but I'll forever be grateful that he introduced me to it. It took me a few months after he left before I was brave enough to come here, but once I did, I found it to be my safe haven.

No one was watching my every move while I was here. No one was judging while I was still fighting to get over him. I could allow myself to grieve for what I'd lost without worrying what everyone else thought.

I had no idea that I was completely in the dark as to what was going on around me back then. I truly believed that Ben had left of his own accord. Naïve? Maybe, but it was what I was led to believe and I didn't really have any reason to question it. I knew the kind of man my dad was. I knew he liked to have everything and everyone under his control, but the little girl inside me who desperately craved for her daddy to be her hero wouldn't allow me to see the severity of it. The evidence was all around me, but I chose to ignore the majority of the warning signs. I truly wanted to believe he had my best interests at heart.

Jenny was devastated that her only son had upped and vanished, and Dad seemed to play the part of the concerned husband and father so well that I never questioned his involvement after I first accused him. I was too broken and lost to question it. Then Joe walked into the office, and he helped put me back together.

As the sun descends, it reflects off something at the bottom of the hill. Squinting my eyes, my stomach jumps into my throat when I see what I assume is Ben's car. I almost laughed when I first saw the bright orange Mitsubishi Warrior parked on Jenny's drive. It's not something I ever would have imagined him driving, but then I remembered it had been six years since I thought I knew him. A lot can change in that time.

Everything about this place starts to make sense.

I never noticed the graveyard below before, but it should have been obvious because I knew where his dad was buried. Ben comes here to be close to him. A giant lump forms in my throat at the thought.

Movement off to the side of the car drags my focus back, and I watch a man who can only be Ben walking towards his car. He stands with his hand on the handle, looking back over his shoulder at where he came from for a few seconds before climbing in.

My heart races. What do I do now? We're too far away to follow him, to do something to try to stop him. Pulling my phone from my pocket, I hesitate for a second but I find his number and put it to my ear, casting aside my concerns and focusing on what Jenny needs.

It doesn't even ring; the automated voice on the other end just tells me that the phone's turned off. Not knowing what else to do, I stand and watch as his car pulls out of the car park. If Jenny's right and he's leaving, then he'll head right out towards the motorway.

I wait for the indicator to flash, and when it does, I'm surprised to see the left one. After a second or two, he pulls away again and heads back into the city.

Blowing out a breath, knowing there's not a lot else to do, I walk back to the taxi. Without thinking, my mum's address falls from my lips when the driver asks me where I'd like to go.

Not feeling up to talking to Jenny, especially if she's still crying, I opt to send her a text explaining that I think he's still about. Hopefully, he'll just head home and they can sort everything out before focusing on the business.

It's dark by the time we get back into the city and pull up outside Mum's building. She still lives in the flat we used to share before I was moved into the show home.

Not knowing I would end up here means that I don't have any keys. I wince as I hit the buzzer, not knowing whether I'll wake her or not. I probably should just go home, but I don't want to be alone and I know that Joe will be out until the early hours.

"Hello?" Mum asks groggily.

"Mum, it's me. Can I come up?" My voice cracks at the end, and I have to fight the entire way up to Mum's flat not to break down.

The second my foot hits the top step and I see her waiting at her front door, I run towards her. She immediately engulfs me in her arms and pulls me inside. The stress, exhaustion and confusion all pour out of me as she walks us towards her living room.

I haven't seen Mum since the funeral.

I guess I've been putting off having this conversation and admitting the truth about what I've done. She knows Ben's back, and she's tried dragging information out of me on the phone, but I've kept my lips sealed. She knows something's going on though. She can read me better than I can myself. She *always* knows.

"Should I go and get us a glass of wine?"

"Yeah," I agree.

While she's busy doing that, I make use of her bathroom, and after splashing my face with water, I feel a little more with it once again.

When I get back, Mum's waiting for me with two giant glasses of wine on the coffee table. "I got the feeling we'd need big ones," she explains with a sympathetic smile, and I can't help but laugh.

Slipping my shoes off, I settle myself into the corner of the sofa and sip at my wine, trying to figure out where the hell to start.

"I'll sit here all night if you need me to, Lauren, but I should warn you that I have work in the morning."

"Sorry," I whisper, a smile twitching at my lips. God, I love my mum. She always manages to say something to lighten the mood.

"It's Dad."

"Oh," Mum says, her eyebrows rising in surprise. I know she was probably expecting me to say Ben's name, and maybe I should start there, but dealing with Dad first seems like the easier option.

"Apparently, he paid Ben off. Dad made him leave." The pain those words cause must be obvious in my voice, but Mum just nods, as if sensing there's more to come. "He'd been blackmailing Erica into cooking the books, and the business is on the verge of bankruptcy. Jenny could lose the house."

"Jesus, Lauren. I really want to tell you that I'm surprised by that but...I was married to your dad for almost ten years."

"I don't even know what to think, Mum. Everything I thought I knew has just been shattered. I thought he left because I was just some kind of twisted fuck-you to Dad. I never expected..." My bottom lip trembles as the reality of how much my dad messed with my life hits me once again. "We could have been happy. We could have..." I don't really want to think of all the things we could have been by now. It's too hard to even consider. "And then there's Erica. He was sleeping with her, Mum. She was at rock bottom after her ex left her, and he took total advantage. She's young enough to be his daughter." My lip curls in disgust. "How could he?"

"I'm so sorry, sweetheart. I always hoped you'd never have to experience that side of your dad."

"Why were you with him?"

"I fell in love, baby. I was young, and he offered me everything I thought I wanted in life. Like I've said many times before, we can't help who we fall in love with. What about Ben? If he didn't leave willingly, where does that leave the two of you? Is he single?"

I open my mouth to respond, but I don't know the answer to that last question. I want to say yes, but knowing that I haven't been entirely honest with him since his reappearance makes me question his own status. "I...uh...I don't know."

"To which question?"

"Either."

"But you're still in love with him. What's the issue?"

"He left me, Mum."

"Yeah, but not by choice, it seems."

"Does it matter? He still went. He could have fought for me. He didn't have to take Dad's money and run. He could have stayed. He could have stayed with me. Hell, he could have taken me *with* him. Anything but leave."

"Has anything happened?" My face flushes bright red, answering her question, and I cast my eyes away, embarrassed.

"What?"

Blowing out a breath, I prepare to tell her what I've done. "He thinks I'm with Joe."

"Why?"

"Because I made it out that way."

"Lauren," she says on a sigh. "What are you doing?"

"I've no fucking clue. I thought I had everything how I wanted it. I was finally in a place where I was enjoying life, and then he turns up and throws everything into chaos. Dad dies, I fall straight back into bed with my stepbrother, and I end up quitting my job." I can't help but laugh at how ridiculous it all sounds.

"You quit? Why?"

I'm silent for a few seconds as I consider how to answer that question. I want to say it's because I don't want to work with Ben, but she'd know that's a lie.

"Look, it's totally your decision, but don't you think you owe it to everyone to stick it out, whether the business makes it or not? If not for Ben or your dad, for Jenny?"

"Us working together isn't a good idea."

"Because you still love him?"

"Yes, okay? Yes, I still love him," I admit, a little louder and more forcefully than I was expecting. "But he left me. He walked out of my life and didn't reappear until my dad died. And what? I'm meant to just carry on like it's six years ago because it's what my heart wants? What about what I deserve?"

"What about what Ben deserves?"

"I'm sorry, what?"

"He hasn't had it easy in all of this either, Lauren."

"Hang on, whose side are you on here?"

"Yours, baby. Always yours. I'm just trying to look at things from both sides. He was forced from the only life he'd known because he fell in love. How easy do you think the last six years have been for him? While you've been here, trying to carry on, he had to totally rebuild his life. You told me before that he left with nothing."

"Nothing but the dirty money Dad gave him."

"That means nothing, and you know it. What's he even been doing for the past six years?"

"I've no idea," I admit quietly. Mum looks at me with disapproval in her eyes. "It hasn't really come up in conversation," I say, trying to defend myself.

"Have you even *had* a conversation?"

My silence says it all. It's true, I guess. When we've been together, we've either been arguing or fucking. I have no clue what his life's been like other than he has what seem to be good friends.

"Do you think maybe you need to sit down with him, get everything out in the open?" I don't respond, because my phone buzzes in my bag. Pulling it out, I smile when I see a picture message from Joe. I quickly swipe to see what he's sent me. It's usually something to show me how much fun he's having, trying to convince me to come and join him. However when the photo loads, my smile drops and my hand trembles.

"Lauren? What's wrong?" Mum's voice sounds a million miles away as I stare down at an image of Ben with a practically naked stripper wrapped around him.

"Motherfucker," I growl, throwing my phone down on the sofa and marching to the other side of the room.

The only thing I can hear is my blood rushing through my ears—that is, until Mum's voice breaks through.

"What's the problem? You're with Joe as far as he's concerned."

CHAPTER THREE

Ben

"BEN." The volume of her calls only intensifies the pounding in my head. "Ben." This time, she accompanies it with knocking.

"Yeah, I'm here," I grate out. My throat's as dry as the fucking Sahara.

"We're meeting Erica at nine. We're going to be late if you don't hurry up."

Rolling over, I drag my eyes open, the morning light burning my sockets, and I have to fight not to pull the duvet over my head and go back to sleep.

Heading to that strip club last night probably

wasn't the best idea, but drowning things out with alcohol and women is the only way I know how.

I've no idea what time I eventually made it home last night, and I only have very vague memories of the journey. Thankfully, I was sensible enough to get in a taxi.

"Ben?" Mum shouts again, correctly assuming that I'm trying to ignore her. "I know you're angry, and I'm sorry, but please, we need to get to the office. There's a lot that needs to be discussed before it's too late."

"Give me ten," I call out.

"Don't forget all your ID for Chris later either," she says, reminding me about our meeting to start the process of getting everything changed over to my name. The prospect of having the weight of not only the business and all its issues but this place on my head is more daunting than I've let anyone see. If I screw this up, it's going to impact a lot of lives.

Sucking in a few deep breaths once I've managed to sit myself on the edge of the bed, I will my stomach to settle. I haven't drunk that much in a long time, but unlike all the previous times I've drunk my problems away, Lauren's face never left me. The image of her in Joe's arms is still right there in front of my eyes, taunting me.

After a few seconds, I pull myself to my feet and stumble towards the en suite. I'm in desperate need of a shower before I grace other humans with my presence.

Mum's at the bottom of the stairs waiting for me. The second my foot hits the ground floor, she walks up to me and throws her arms around my shoulders. I tense. I'm still angry with her for interfering, but I don't have it in me to turn her away right now.

"I'm so glad you didn't leave."

"Trust me, it was close."

"Where did you go?"

"It doesn't matter." Placing my hands on her shoulders, I prise her away from me. There's no way I'm telling her about going to see Dad; it'll only make her ask questions that I'm not prepared to answer. "Come on, Erica will be waiting."

"Where's your car?" Mum asks when she notices it's missing.

"Outside the strip club," I mutter to her surprise, if her gasp is anything to go by.

"You went to a strip club?" The line between her brows deepens, disapproval written all over her face.

"Yes, Mum. I went to a strip club. I found the woman I'm in love with in another man's arms, and I needed a distraction. Do you have a problem with that?" I regret snapping the moment tears pool in her eyes, but I'm really not in the mood to have my bad decisions questioned right now.

Everyone's busy when we get to the office, but it doesn't stop Betty from dropping whatever she's doing and running towards the kitchen to make us coffee the second we enter.

"Give us ten minutes, yeah?" Mum says to Erica as we pass, then she shuts the door behind both of us once we're in the office.

I don't bother waiting to see where she's going to sit. I go straight for the chair behind the desk…my chair. What I don't expect is for Mum to turn her determined stare on me.

"What?"

"I need to know that you're in this for the long haul, Ben. This business needs someone who's going to be serious, not someone who's going to want to run at the first sign of trouble. Hell knows, we've already had enough of that. What we need to do here isn't going to be easy. It's going to take hard work and dedication, and if you're not the man for the job, then I have no problem with finding someone who is."

My eyebrows rise in surprise. It's been years since I've heard Mum talk with such conviction. She and Dad ran this place like a tight ship when I was a kid, but after he died and Nick took over, it was like all her fight just disappeared. If she'd kept just a little of her tenacity, maybe we wouldn't be in this position right now.

"I can do it," I say, spinning on the chair to power up the computer.

"What was that?" Her eyebrow quirks and her hand lands on her hip.

"I can do it."

"I know you can, but do you *want* to?"

It might have been inevitable that I end up here, but all my life it truly was the only thing I wanted. I never considered any other career options. I'd watched my granddad and dad build this business, and from as early as I could remember, I was hungry to join them. I always expected that I'd get to work beside Dad, for a few years at least. I never would have imagined that I'd be taking over at such a crucial time for the business, but that's even more reason for me to give this my all. This is where I need to be, because there's not a chance in hell that I'm going to allow what the men before me built to disappear as if it never existed.

I glance over Mum's shoulder at where all the office staff are behind the wall. It's the reminder I need that this isn't just about me. This is about them, their families, their futures.

"I want to. I always have," I admit.

"Good. Just remember that, because what's coming your way is going to be hard." I nod and our eye contact holds. "If we're going to dig our way out of the mess he left behind, you've got some tough decisions to make."

"We, you mean?"

"No. I mean *you*. This place is yours now. You're the boss. You say jump, and we all ask how high. The success of this place is yours to create."

"Jesus." The weight of what's been placed on my shoulders suddenly feels heavier than anything else I've dealt with in my life.

"Ready?"

"Can't wait." It might sound sarcastic, but Mum knows I'm taking this seriously—or at least I hope she does.

Mum turns when there's a knock at the door and Betty comes walking in with two mugs in her hands.

"Thank you, Betty." She smiles politely at us before scurrying from the room again. "Erica?"

Getting up from my seat, I walk over and join Mum at the meeting desk at the other end of the room.

Erica takes the seat next to me, her face tight with the stress of keeping this place going.

"Where's Lauren?" Erica asks, pointing out the obvious.

All eyes turn to me, and I hesitate to answer because it's my fault she's not here. "She's...uh..."

"She handed in her notice last night, effective immediately."

"What?" Erica shrieks. "She can't do that. We need her."

"I think Ben's got his work cut out for him to get her back." Mum's stare turns on me, and I groan in response.

"That's a work in progress, but it's not our most vital issue right now." Eyes widen at my quick dismissal of Lauren's position here, but I can't dwell on the fact that she'd rather not be here right now. "We need to nail down what work we've got, what we've got coming up, and we seriously need to look at staffing. I hate to say it, but we're going to need to cut costs, and getting rid of any dead wood seems like the best place to start."

"So it's probably a good thing then that Steve's retiring at the end of the month?"

"Seriously? No, that's not a good thing. We need someone to run the jobs we've got." Steve has been the main contracts manager at Johnson & Son's as long as I can remember. He's absolutely not one of the people I was considering that needed to go.

"Okay, right... We're going to need to sit down separately then, and make a plan of action. For now, though, let's look at the jobs."

We spend hours strategizing and trying to come up with a plan to save as much money and as many jobs as possible. The last thing I want to do is take over and make a load of people redundant, but with our financial situation, I'm not sure what else to do.

"There's one more thing I wanted to talk to you about," Mum says once Erica's gone back to her desk.

"Shoot."

"I think it might be worth looking at different premises. Maybe move a little farther out of the city. This place is quite a cost every month."

"No."

"Ben," she says with a sigh. "I know how important this place is to you. Trust me, I understand. It's like a second home to me, but we need to think with our heads, not our hearts, if we want to turn this around."

Ripping my eyes from hers, I look around the office. I've got so many happy memories of Dad in this place. I can't imagine moving the business somewhere else, but I know Mum's right. Now's not the time to be sentimental.

"I'll start looking for options."

"I've got faith in you, baby."

I nod, not wanting to get into that kind of conversation right now. My head is still pounding from last night's whiskey, and now it's spinning with everything I need to do here. Add the fact that I've just agreed to visit our biggest site right now to see how it's going, into the mix, and I'm ready to call it a day. It's not that I don't want to go to the site—I'm actually quite excited to see it as the project sounds incredible—but the problem is who's running it.

Pulling up to the old factory on the outskirts of Kensington, I sit back and appreciate the Victorian architecture hiding behind the cage of scaffolding. This building is going to be stunning once its restoration is complete. The luxury apartments inside are going to be worth a pretty penny. This is our most lucrative project currently running, so it's vital that we pull as much out of it as possible. That means I need to be on top of everything, as well as working closely with the site manager...Joe.

Reaching behind me, I grab my high-visibility jacket and hardhat from the van I borrowed, as my car's still parked somewhere by the strip club. Telling myself that I need to be civil and polite, I head off to find the man in charge.

There are people everywhere, both inside and outside the building. I know from looking at the schedule back in the office that they're on a tight timeline to get the works complete, but still, it seems a little crazy.

Hearing from a couple of our guys that Joe had gone up to the roof, I find a ladder and start climbing.

When I eventually get to the top of the scaffolding, I find him talking to a couple of others by a broken section of tiles.

I've only taken a couple of steps towards them when his head snaps up and his eyes find mine. His expression hardens and only gets angrier the closer I get. It takes a few seconds for the guys he's with to notice, but when they do, they stop talking and turn my way.

"Ben, mate, it's so good to see you. I heard you were back."

"Will," I say, nodding to a guy I used to consider my friend. "How's it going?"

"Good, good. This one's a bit of a hard taskmaster though," he says, nodding to Joe.

"I'm glad he's keeping you on your toes. Do you mind? Joe and I have some things to discuss."

"Sure thing, boss man...you are the boss now, right?"

"I am, so I suggest you get to work."

"He used to be fun, you know," Will calls over his shoulder as he and the other guy I don't recognise head towards the ladder.

Every muscle in my body is tense as we stand in silence, waiting to see who's going to speak.

In the end, I break first. "I don't know how much you know about the current situation with the company," I say, assuming that Lauren will have filled him in, "but needless to say, this is our biggest job right now and it's imperative that it's as successful as possible. That means you and I will be working closely together in the coming weeks. So unless you intend on finding a new job, I suggest you get used to the fact that I'm going to be in your life whether you like it or not."

"Until things get too hard and you run again," he mutters.

"Excuse me?" I want to believe I misheard that, but I know I didn't.

"You heard. You don't belong here, and you know it. You made your bed six years ago, so I'd recommend you go back to wherever it is and lie in it."

"I'm not here to discuss my life with you or to argue over what's mine."

"That's good, because nothing here is yours," he spits. Red-hot anger races through my veins and my teeth grind in an attempt not to put my hands on him.

Stepping up to me, his fists clench at his sides. A smug grin twitches at my lips. Good, I'm getting to him. "You and I both know that's not true. There's only ever been one man for Lauren, and that man's me. Just give it time. You'll see." I know I shouldn't be rising to this, but the look on his fucking face is too much to deny. He thinks he's winning here, but he has no understanding of the thing between Lauren and I. Hell, most of the time I don't understand it. But it's there and it's very real, even after all these years.

"Remind yourself of that when you're lying in a cold and empty bed tonight and her hot little body is wrapped around mine."

"Fuck you," I spit, wrapping the fabric of his shirt in my hand and pushing him back against the scaffolding. My chest heaves as I stare deep into his eyes, trying to rid the image of the two of them together once again. "She doesn't want you. Not really. You were just a filler." His eyes narrow slightly at my blatant disregard for their relationship. It's obvious he cares for her, loves her even, but it will never be a match for what the two of us have, and I'm pretty sure that, deep down, he must know that. He knows she's been fucking sleeping with me for fuck's sake—of course he knows.

"Like the strippers are to you?"

"What?" My stomach knots and my hand loosens in surprise. Stepping back, he manages to put some space between us.

"That's right. She knows all about what you got up to last night, so don't try the fucking innocent act with me. You were all over those women. How do you think that made her feel when you say you only want her?"

"Motherfucker." I launch myself at him, but before we connect, there's an almighty crash below us, and the world falls out from under me.

CHAPTER FOUR

Lauren

I ENDED up staying at Mum's last night. By the time we'd analysed the situation with Ben from every angle possible, I'd had too much wine and it was too late to faff around getting a taxi when I could just stay in my old room.

I stayed in bed long after Mum got up and left for work. The rollercoaster of emotions over the last few days have left me exhausted, so I made the most of the peace and quiet, and of course the fact that I'm now unemployed.

I've had a job since the week I turned sixteen, so

not having somewhere to go, something to do or anyone waiting on me is the weirdest feeling. Emailing Ben my resignation was a bit of a spur of the moment decision, but after what happened out in the car park, I just knew it wasn't a good idea for us to spend time together. Was resigning from my job crazy? Maybe. But I couldn't—I still can't—see any other way. Seeing him after all this time is so hard. Seeing the longing in his eyes every time he so much as glances my way damn near rips my heart out.

I desperately want to believe the words I keep telling everyone, that we're over, that I don't care about him anymore. But they're all lies. I always knew I'd never stopped loving him, but seeing him again made it so fucking obvious.

Feeling lost, I drive to a spa in the hope that treating myself might make me feel slightly better. I book myself in for a facial, back massage and mani-pedi. I might feel like I'm dying inside with everything that's going on, so I guess I should at least try to look like I'm surviving on the outside.

Resting back in the relaxation room in my white fluffy robe after my first two treatments, I allow the soothing music and the soft scent of the candles to wash through me and try to push out all the stress.

It's all going well until my phone starts vibrating

in my pocket. Seeing Erica's name, I pause before answering, knowing that she's probably only ringing to bend my ear about leaving.

The call rings off, but no sooner has the screen gone dark than it lights up again. My curiosity gets the better of me and I swipe to answer.

"Lauren?" Erica asks in a rush before it's even to my ear.

"Yeah, what's up?"

"There's been an accident." My heart drops into my stomach hearing those words.

"Ben?"

"Ben and Joe. They're on their way to Chelsea and Westminster Hospital."

Jumping from the chair, I rush towards the changing room. My robe's been discarded before I've got anywhere near my locker in my need to get to them. "I'm on my way."

My entire body trembles in fear as I try to get myself dressed. It takes me longer than it usually would, and I get more and more frustrated at myself for my inability to keep a cool head right now.

I don't know anything. They could be fine. They are fine, I repeat, trying to stay relaxed and focused on what I need to do.

The drive to the hospital is a total blur. I've no

idea how I got here in one piece. For all I know, I jumped every red light and cut up every car I came in contact with.

It's the longest twenty minutes of my life before I walk through to the accident and emergency waiting room.

"Lauren," a female voice calls the second I step towards the reception desk, but everything's a blur. I've no idea what happened or if they're alive. My heart starts to race, and I fight to suck in breaths as the reality of the situation starts to hit me. "Lauren."

Everything around me fades to black. Hands touch me, but I've no idea what they're doing. The only thing I feel is sheer panic. My heart races and my chest heaves to drag in the oxygen it needs.

He has to be okay. This can't really be it for us. He has to be okay.

"Lauren, it's okay, sweetheart." The sound of Jenny's soothing voice eventually breaks through the haze. When I come back to myself, I realise that I'm sitting on one of the reception chairs with Jenny, the woman from reception, and a kind looking nurse all staring at me.

My heart is still racing, but I feel like I can actually breathe again.

"It's okay, love. You just had a wee panic attack,"

the nurse says like it's nothing to worry about. "Call if you need anything."

Nodding at her, I continue to focus on my breathing as she and the receptionist head back to work.

"What's happened?"

"There was an accident on site. A lorry hit the scaffolding and Ben and Joe were at the top."

"At the top?" I screech. "Are they...Are they...?" I can't bring myself to say the words.

"I've no idea." It's only now that I see the fear in Jenny's eyes.

Jenny takes my hand in hers, and we sit back in silence, both lost in our own thoughts and prayers. I've never been even slightly religious, but I'll do whatever it takes right now to ensure that I see them both again. I've already lost six years with Ben. I can't even comprehend—

"Are they okay?" Erica asks, rushing into reception a while later followed by Betty, who's trying her best to keep up.

"We don't know."

Betty pulls Jenny into her arms, and it's the final straw because she sobs on her shoulder. I know she was trying to be strong for me, and I appreciate it, but I'd rather she didn't keep it all inside.

I watch, feeling totally useless as Erica marches up to the reception desk and demands to know what's going on. The receptionist is busy trying to calm her down when a familiar figure walks through the door.

"Joe," I cry, racing towards him and throwing my arms around his shoulders. He winces and sucks in a sharp breath.

"Shit, I'm sorry. Are you okay? What Happened? Where's Ben?"

Gently pulling me back to him, he slowly walks us towards where the others are not so patiently waiting to hear more. It's only once we've sat down that I get a good look at him. He's got a black eye and swelling down the side of his face. He's clutching onto his ribs with a scratched and bruised arm.

"Shouldn't you be in there?" Jenny asks, concern filling her voice.

"I'm fine," he says, but he looks anything but. "It looks worse than it is. Ben broke my fall."

"Is he...?"

"I don't know, sweets. He was taken in a different ambulance, but he looked to be in a bad way." A sob bubbles up my throat and Joe pulls me into him as Jenny cries behind me.

"Yes. I'm sorry, I really can only talk to immediate family."

"I'm his...sister," I say with a wince. It's the first and only time I've ever referred to myself as that, and it feels wrong.

"Okay, well both of you come through then."

Joe reluctantly lets me go and I thread my arm through Jenny's as we follow the doctor through the doors.

We sit together as the doctor explains how Ben fell from the top of the scaffolding. Thankfully, the panels below broke their fall, but Ben had a potentially critical blow to the head as well as fracturing his arm and four ribs. He was unconscious when he arrived and they've now got him sedated until they can get him a MRI scan to assess any swelling on the brain. My hands tremble with fear. Although he's stable right now, things can change very quickly with brain injuries.

"Can we see him?" Jenny asks.

"Of course. But just the two of you. Follow me, I'll take you through."

My heart races as the doctor opens the door and the end of a hospital bed is revealed. Tears burn my eyes and I swallow down the giant lump in my throat as I prepare to see Ben lying there, totally helpless.

"Oh my god," I sob the second his body comes into view.

Jenny rushes forward to him, but I stay frozen to the spot, just staring at his lifeless body. My vision starts to blur again and I reach out to the doorframe for support as my heart races too fast. The anger that's been simmering within me since seeing the photo of him in the strip club last night collides with my panic.

The only time I've really spent in a hospital before today was the day Dad died, and that was only to collect his stuff. His heart attack hit him while he was driving. Thankfully, he knew something wasn't right, pulled over and called for an ambulance. But he never made it to the hospital. He crashed in the ambulance and they weren't able to revive him. I knew at the time that I wouldn't be able to cope seeing him hooked up to machines, but I think that might have been easier than what I'm witnessing right now.

"Lauren," Jenny breathes, racing over and helping me towards one of the chairs next to Ben's bed.

"I don't think I can do this. I don't think I can do this," I chant as she lowers me down.

"Yes you can. You can do this because Ben needs

you to." Her voice is strong and steady and shows me that she's more capable in a crisis that I think I ever gave her credit for. I never realised how smothered she was by Dad, but it's only in the days since he's been gone that I'm starting to see the real woman that was hiding behind his control.

"He's quite heavily sedated, but you can talk to him. Hearing your voices might help," the doctor says from the corner of the room.

Once Jenny's happy that I'm okay, she turns to her son.

"Ben, baby, Lauren and I are here. Everything's going to be okay."

A sob erupts from my throat at her words. Standing, I turn to leave. I'm not strong enough for this.

"Lauren, he needs you." Jenny's words stop my progress to the door. "If you still care about him at all, you won't walk out that door."

Like a movie, images of our time together play out in my mind. The fun we had before he was ripped away from me. I remember the way he used to look at me with such awe in his eyes, the gentleness of his touch, his thoughtfulness. But then I'm once again filled with the emptiness that almost engulfed me when he left, and the anger from knowing what he was doing last night while I was breaking once again.

Letting out a sigh, I know what I need to do. This isn't about me and my fears or anger. This is about Ben and his fight.

Turning back, I take the seat closest to him and slide my hand into his. The callus that used to feel rough against my skin is gone, reminding me that I've no idea what he's been doing for work—or anything, really—since he's been gone.

Jenny nods, and a very small smile quirks the corner of her lips. She moves the second chair to his other side, and I sit in silence as she talks nonsense to him.

"We should probably let the others know what's going on."

"I'll go. You should stay with him. When he wakes, you're the one he's going to want."

"No, I—" One look from Jenny and all arguments leave me.

Leaning forward, she presses a kiss to Ben's forehead and silently leaves the room. The only sounds are that of the machines Ben's hooked up to and my racing heart.

My head's such a mess that I have no clue what I should be feeling right now. He threw me for a loop with his reappearance, but I never expected any of it to be this hard. I really thought Ben had gone for good, and when I got the call to tell me that Dad had passed away, I pushed any thoughts of him reappearing to the back of my mind.

The changes in him were obvious: his hair had gone, his muscles had grown and his tattoos were everywhere. I didn't stand a chance with his good looks all those years ago, and I knew if he was sticking around that I was going to have a fight on my hands. It's not just what's on the outside though, and I can try to convince myself that it is until I'm blue in the face. There's something inside him that just calls to me on a level I've never experienced with anyone else. Six years might have passed, but when he stared at me that first day, that feeling, that connection...it was still there, and it was stronger than ever.

I don't think I've ever been this scared. I barely made it through the heartache of him leaving before. I know for a fact that, if I open my heart to him again, I will not survive the consequences when he changes his mind.

I stare down at my hand in his as I think about everything that's happened since he reappeared...all the mistakes I've made. I told myself that I wouldn't go there again, that I wouldn't allow him to touch me, but I did. I broke every single fucking rule I made when he walked out of my life. I broke every fucking promise I made to Joe, and I can see his disappointment every time I look into his eyes. As angry as I am at him for breaking down the barriers I'd put up, I'm angrier at myself. I never thought of myself as weak, but knowing now how quickly I caved to him makes me think that I just might be.

That's why it won't happen again. I need to think about myself and my future. I want one where I'm not constantly either nursing the broken heart he's so good at leaving me with, or wondering if today's the day that he's going to leave again. I deserve better than that. I deserve someone who loves and protects me the way he promised all those years ago.

"You promised," I sob, my emotions getting the better of me. "You promised that, no matter what, you'd protect me. But you walked away and caused me more pain than anyone else had the power to cause. I fucking loved you, Ben, with all my heart, and you just stomped all over it like it meant nothing to you." Dropping my head into my hands, I continue to cry for everything I've lost.

Now knowing he left because of my dad doesn't make any of it any better. Ben didn't have to do what he was told. He could have stayed and fought, but he chose to follow orders and leave.

Sitting back when my tears have subsided, I refuse to look at him. I'm angry with him for so much that I don't even know which bit to start analysing. All I know is that, right now, I love and hate him in equal measures. No matter how much I might want to walk out that door right now, I can't. I can't leave him here to fight this alone.

I tell myself that I'll stay by his side until he's pulled through, but then I'm gone, and whatever there might be between us is done. I can walk away knowing that he's okay, and I can properly make a fresh start this time.

CHAPTER FIVE

Ben

WHISPERED VOICES FILL MY MIND, but I can't make out who they belong to or even what they're saying.

I fight to open my eyes, to find out where I am, but it's like I'm in a dream and everything's just out of reach. Like I'm running towards a never-ending goal.

Just when the voices start to sound familiar somehow, everything goes black again.

The next time I hear something, it's just one soft

and familiar voice…but although it's soft, there's unmistakable anger within it.

What's going on? Where am I?

I fight to focus, to hear just a couple of the words that are being said, but everything's a haze. Before long, everything's gone again.

"You should go home and get some rest. It's been almost twenty-four hours." It's the first time I've heard a voice I haven't recognised. Panic starts to build, not knowing where I am or what's going on, but no matter how hard I try, I can't open my damn eyes.

"No, I want to be here just in case." My heart jumps. That's Lauren. Wherever I am, she's here.

"He's going to be fine. The MRI showed very little swelling. It's just a case of waiting for him to wake up."

I want to tell them that I'm here, that I'm awake, but I can't force my throat to work, and I can't feel my limbs move.

"Once he's awake, I'll leave."

No, I try to scream but nothing happens. I don't want her to leave. She's exactly where she should be. I just need to tell her.

Then, everything's gone once again.

"Are you sure that's a good idea?" That's Mum's voice. I'd know it anywhere.

"Yes. I just need a break, Jenny. This week has been..." Lauren trails off. *This week has been what? What am I missing?*

"I know, sweetheart, but he's going to need you when he wakes up."

"He'll be fine. The doctors have said so."

"Lauren, don't be like that."

"Like what? He made it very clear that he doesn't need me. He's coped for the last six years, so I'm sure he'll be fine after this."

Mum sighs but she doesn't say any more, and everything falls silent.

"HAVE YOU BOOKED IT? Awesome. What time's the flight? Heathrow? Can you forward me the details?" It takes a while, but I figure Lauren must be on the phone. "Yeah, they're going to wake him up if he hasn't already. Yeah, it'll be fine. Yes, I'm sure." Frustration starts to fill her voice at whatever the person she's talking to is saying. "Yeah. Okay. Yeah. See you soon, bye."

Lauren groans before the side of the bed dips.

"Why is this so hard?" she complains. I'm desperate to do something to make it better for her.

Then, the most incredible thing happens. Tingles run up my arm as she slips her hand into mine. If I were able to, I might cry with delight, but it seems my body is still utterly useless.

I put everything I have into it, and eventually I swear my fingers move.

"Ben? Ben, can you hear me?" I'm so desperate to reply, but nothing happens. "Squeeze my hand if you can hear me." The effort it takes just to move my fingers is exhausting, but I manage it. "Oh my god, you can." She's silent for a few seconds before she speaks again, and as glad as I am to hear her voice, the words aren't what I'd like.

"This is fucking karma for all the bullshit you've caused. You know that, right? Do you have any idea what you've put us through? Maybe you should have left the other day. You might have made it easier on all of us."

I've no clue what she's talking about, and I rack my brain for memories, but there's nothing there. No reason why I might be lying here like a fucking vegetable with her shouting at me.

I've no idea if she says any more, because I fade away again.

"I swear he could hear me. He squeezed my hand," Lauren explains.

"It could still be hours yet. Please, come home, sweets." The sound of Joe's voice brings a memory of us to the surface. We were outside somewhere, and I was getting in his face. I remember being angry and wanting nothing more than to wipe the smirk off his face.

"Not until he wakes."

"You do know that if he wakes up with you here, he's going to get the wrong idea? Do you really want to encourage him after you only just got rid of him?"

He really thinks their little stunt was enough for me to forget about Lauren?

As they continue bickering, more and more of my body starts to come back to me. Being able to wiggle my toes is the best feeling in the world after being numb for fuck knows how long.

Her hand is in mine once again, and my lips threaten to break into a smile. I bet Joe's fucking pissed with his girl sitting beside my bed and holding my hand.

"I told Jenny I would get you to leave and at least have a shower."

"How many times? I'm not leaving until he's awake."

"Fine. Well...call me if you need anything."

"I will." The sound of him giving her a kiss has every muscle in my body tightening, but then the door shuts and silence descends.

"Ben, come on." She sounds exhausted. "It's time for you to wake up, baby." Warmth fills my insides. "Let me see those beautiful blue eyes. Show me that you're okay." Her words are sincere.

I give it everything I've got, and eventually I manage to drag my eyelids open so just the tiniest bit of light seeps in.

"Oh my god. Ben? Ben, come on, baby, look at me."

The light is so bright that my eyes start running the moment I manage to open them further. I want to see her more than anything, but right now she's just a blur of blonde hair.

"Can you see me?"

I manage to shake my head slightly and, after blinking a few times, my vision clears and I'm blessed with the most incredible sight.

Lauren.

She might look pale and exhausted, but I don't care because she's right here.

I stare at her, taking in every feature and

committing it to memory just in case my eyes don't work again.

I open my mouth to say something, but nothing comes out. It's like I've been on a week-long bender with how dry it is. Although, to be fair, my head hurts pretty bad so maybe that's what happened. Did I drink myself into oblivion?

The warmth of her palm against my rough cheek feels like heaven. "It's okay. I'm here. My god, it's so good to be able to look into your eyes." The relief she's feeling is evident in her voice, and it makes me think that maybe this isn't the hangover from hell. She genuinely looks terrified. "What do you need? Can I get you anything?" I try to speak again to tell her that that she's the only thing I need, but it doesn't work.

"Here, sip this." A straw is placed between my lips and I manage to sip a little water. It does the trick, because I can swallow again.

"W-where am I?" It comes out as a hoarse whisper, but at least it came out.

"In the hospital." Her voice has lost the concern that was there only moments ago. It's hard, like I remember from when she was talking to Mum.

"Why?"

"Because you reappeared and turned everything

to shit," she snaps. "What the fuck were you thinking, going after Joe like that? He's done nothing to you. He didn't deserve that. I'm so fucking mad at you," she fumes, getting up and pacing the room. I'm a little whiplashed from her sudden mood change.

"You just turn up and flip my world upside down. Do you have any idea how long it took me to get my life back on track after you left? No, how could you, because you just fucked off without looking back. You were a fucking pussy, you know that? One little threat and you fucking ran. I thought I meant more to you than that. I thought you loved me. I sure as shit know I did you.

"Look what good that did me." She throws her arms up as she continues pacing.

I watch her every move, more confused than ever.

"I said I'd stay until you were awake." She grabs her jacket from the chair, and I panic.

"No. No, please, don't go." I'm fucking exhausted but that doesn't mean I won't do whatever it takes to make her stay with me right now. "Please, Lauren." My exhaustion and emotions collide and my eyes fill with tears. I should be embarrassed about the fact that I'm about five seconds away from crying like a baby, but I don't give a fuck. Lauren is the one person on the planet I can truly be myself with, and if that means she sees me at my worst right now, then so be it. "Please." It comes out as a whisper this time, and it's enough to stop her.

She turns her tired eyes on me, and the sight is enough for guilt to flow through me at asking her to do this. What everyone else has been saying to her has been right. She needs to rest.

She stares at me for two seconds before she steps forward. I breathe a sigh of relief as she gently sits on the edge of my bed and takes my hand in hers.

"I'm...I'm sorry. That was...uncalled for. I was just so scared, Ben. I thought I was going to lose you. We had no idea if you were dead or alive, and I just couldn't even imagine what I would do if—"

"Hey, it's okay. I'm okay."

"And then Joe told me what happened, and I was so mad at you." My previous elation over her concern is clouded by confusion. "What did I do?"

"You don't remember?"

My eyelids get heavier and heavier as we stare at each other, and eventually I lose the fight. Everything goes black, and I've no idea if she stays or goes.

WHEN I COME BACK AROUND, I feel much more normal. I mean, my head pounds like a motherfucker, my throat's dry once again, and every muscle in my body aches, but I can open my eyes, feel every limb, and more importantly, I can move. A little sliver of positivity creeps in. Well, that is, until I look to the chair beside my bed and find it empty.

She's gone.

I shouldn't be surprised. It's what I deserve after what I've put her through, but I still hoped that she'd be here.

"Ah, he's awake," Mum says, walking in with a coffee.

"Where's Lauren?"

"Nice to see you too, son. You gave us quite a fright there."

"Where is she?"

"She's having some well deserved time to herself. She's been sitting by your side for the last twenty-four hours."

I've been out for twenty-four hours? I push the thought aside, because that isn't important right now. What is important is the fact that despite telling me she hates me and rubbing Joe in my face, she sat here with me the whole time.

"I need to find her."

Relief floods me when I go to swing my legs from the bed and they actually follow instruction. That is, until the searing pain from my ribs stops any further movement. I suck in a sharp breath. The agony is the only thing I can focus on, and its ferocity has tears stinging my eyes. "Fuck."

"Ben, you're in hospital. You can't just get up and walk out."

"Watch me," I wince through the pain.

"Ben, please. You need to be checked over before you do anything stupid."

"I'm fine," I lie. Moving right now is the hardest fucking thing I've ever done, but my need to get to Lauren is stronger. I go to move my hand to rip the cannula out, but my arm's heavy as fuck. When I look down, I understand why. It's wrapped in a solid white cast. Jesus, how much of me is broken?

"Ah, Mr. Johnson, it's nice to see you awake." A nurse and doctor come strolling in, looking delighted to see me. "Going somewhere?" the doctor asks, concern in his eyes.

"Yes. I need to see someone."

"How about we do our tests first, hey?"

"I haven't got ti—"

"Ben," Mum snaps. That, along with the looks in

both the nurse and doctor's eyes, means I take a step back and sit on the edge of the bed.

"Just make it quick."

I watch the clock tick around as they check everything that needs checking and poke and prod me until they're happy with my progress. I told them I was fine and just needed some painkillers, but they wouldn't have it.

"We'd like to keep you in another night, just to monitor you."

"No," I say getting out of bed. "Do I have clothes here?"

"Ben, I really think you should—"

"Fighting me isn't going to work. I'm not sitting around in here. I'm fine."

"You've been unconscious for a day. You're anything but fine."

"I need her, Mum."

"I know you do, but now's not the time. She'll be gone–"

"Gone–" A memory hits me. Her one-sided conversation about flights and Heathrow airport. "Shit."

Jumping from the bed, pain from my ribs makes my breath catch and my head spins. I lift my arm, hoping to ease the pounding in my head, but the cast collides with my forehead, knocking me back to the bed.

None of this is going to stop me. I need to find her before it's too late.

Finding a little cupboard next to the bed, I pull the door open, not giving two shits that I'm flashing Mum in my open-back hospital gown.

"Ben, please be sensible. If the doctor says you should stay, then you should." Her warnings go unheard as I pull some fresh clothes from a bag and tug them on.

"Where's she going?" I demand.

Mum's face pales when she realises that I know. "I don't know."

"Don't give me that. Tell me. Make up for sabotaging me the other night."

"Honestly, I don't know. I told her not to tell me so I wouldn't be put in this position. All I know is that she and Danni are going away for a few days."

Fucking hell.

Grabbing the bag and the few belongings I have, I storm from the room and then the hospital.

The sun's setting when I drag my broken body out of the main entrance, and I realise for the first time that I lost a whole day of my life in a hospital bed. I eventually find a taxi idling at the entrance whose driver is willing to give me a lift. Fuck knows what I look like right now. If his wide eyes are anything to go by, probably like I've been hit by a truck.

Scaffolding...A memory of being on top of the scaffolding on site, talking to Joe, emerges. We were arguing, no surprise there.

The taxi pulls up beside my car, which is still parked up by the strip club, and the last piece of the puzzle falls into place. This is what we were arguing about. Joe knew I was here, which means so does Lauren. Christ only knows what kind of stories he made up after finding me there.

I pay the driver, dig my keys from the bottom of my bag, and climb into my car. Everything aches, and the pain in my ribs almost has me crying out.

I just about manage the short drive to the office. Thankfully, it's my right arm that's in a cast; I'd never manage this if it was my left. I practically drag my body up the last few stairs, desperate to rest. The thought of lying in that hospital bed suddenly seems appealing, but I know this is what I need to do.

Thankfully, the office is deserted when I stumble through the front door, pull out her chair and sit gingerly at her desk. I've no idea if this is going to give me the information I need, but it's my only chance of finding out.

Powering up her computer, I try a few possible passwords, but nothing lets me in. Groaning in frustration, I pick up the phone and call our IT support.

Twenty minutes later and I've got access to her account as well as her emails. Being the boss sure does have some perks.

She's got loads of unread emails, so the only one that's actually been read stands out like a sore thumb.

Subject: Rome, here we come!

Opening the email I discover that Danni's forwarded the itinerary as Lauren requested. Scanning through the information to find out when their flight leaves, my heart drops.

"Fuck."

Jumping from the seat, I cry out as pain shoots in all directions. Knowing that driving myself will take longer, I order a taxi. I don't know what I'm going to have to do when I get to the airport, but I somehow remember to grab my passport that I'd left in my desk ready for the meeting with Chris. Getting back down the stairs is a bigger challenge than I was expecting. I clutch my ribs, but every time I take a step down, my body feels like it's going to split in two.

The taxi's already waiting by the time I get to the front doors. I must look as pathetic as I feel, because the driver actually gets out to come and help me.

"I'm fine, thanks," I grunt.

After giving him my destination, I sit back and allow my head to drop to the headrest. I intend to just shut my eyes for a moment in the hope the painkillers will start kicking in, but when I open them again, we're pulling up to the drop-off area at Heathrow.

"You okay, mate?" the driver asks, looking back at me in the rear-view mirror.

I mumble a polite response as I dig some cash from my wallet and pass it over. "Thank you."

Standing in front of the colossal terminal, I'm not sure I can put another foot in front of the other. I knew this was a stupid idea the second I walked out of the hospital, but the magnitude of the challenge ahead of me now seems very real. There are thousands of people inside that building—what really are my chances of finding the one I want?

Deciding that she's worth the risk, I drag my foot from the ground and haul my aching body inside and towards the British Airways desks.

"I'm looking for someone who's scheduled to board your flight to Rome in thirty minutes."

The woman stares at me like I've got three heads. I know I probably look like a crazy man, but I don't care. I need to get to Lauren before it's too late.

"I'm sorry, Sir, but the gate has already been called."

I think for a second. "Give me a ticket."

"I'm sorry."

"Are there any seats available on the plane?"

"Uh...yes."

"Great, I'll have one."

The woman's eyes widen, but she clicks on her computer and, in a few seconds, she's asking for payment. I cough to cover my surprise when she tells me the cost. Lauren's worth it and then some, so I hand my card over willingly.

"It's departing from gate forty-three. You're going to need to hurry." She glances down at my cast and then to where I'm holding my ribs. "Would you like some assistance?

I hate the idea of being treated like an invalid, but the pain radiating through my body soon gives the answer I need. "That would be great, thank you."

She lifts the phone to her ear and is soon looking back up at me with sympathy filling her eyes. "Someone will be here to pick you up in just a second. Good luck, sir."

As promised, a guy on a golf buggy type thing pulls to a stop in front of me. "Your carriage awaits, sir. Where to?"

I rattle off the gate number and carefully climb on board. He wastes no time in putting his foot down and we speed off through the crowds at a fucking snails pace. The longer I sit there, the more my frustration grows. It probably would have been faster to fucking walk.

I breathe a sigh of relief when the gate number comes into view. I pray that she'll still be in there and that I'm not going to have to say what I need to on the plane with hundreds of witnesses.

The moment I turn to enter the gate, I see her. She's standing with Danni, just about to hand their tickets over to board.

"Lauren, wait."

CHAPTER SIX

Lauren

AS HARD AS it was to walk away from Ben, I knew it was what I needed to do. Danni had been talking about us getting away for a few days for weeks, and when the doctors confirmed that Ben would most probably make a full recovery and be fully awake within the next twelve hours, I knew it was time. It wasn't healthy for me to be sitting beside his bed, waiting for him to wake up. It was safe while he was asleep. I could cry and tell him all the things I was too scared to when he was awake. I could pretend that all the bullshit hadn't happened and that things were just like they once were between us as I held his hand and allowed his warmth to soothe me...see, unhealthy.

I told Danni I didn't care where we went, just that I needed some time away, and she came through within minutes, telling me that she'd booked us a few days in Rome. Of course I'm excited. I'm not only about to get to spend some much needed girl time with my best friend, but I'm going to be able to explore a new place while I attempt to push home and Ben to the back of my mind.

With Danni back at uni to do her Masters degree, we haven't spent much time together recently. There's so much that's happened in the last few weeks that she doesn't know about. My time has pretty much been taken up by family, Ben and Joe. I feel guilty that I haven't filled her in on all the huge revelations I've discovered. I'm also desperate to get her take on everything. She's always been the slightly more straight-headed one out of the two of us.

"Wait, so you're telling me that I shut myself in my flat for a few days to write an essay and missed all this? No wonder Joe demanded we go out the other night. Jesus, Lauren," Danni says when I finish explaining about what Dad did to both Ben and Erica. "So, where are things at with you and Ben?

Please tell me you jumped him the second he reappeared, because if you don't mind me saying, that boy's only got hotter. He looked like sex on a stick when Joe pointed him out the other night at the stri—shit."

"It's okay. I was mortified when Joe sent the picture, but I've realised since that Ben wasn't really doing anything wrong. It's not like we're—"

"Joe sent a picture?"

"Yeah."

"Why?"

"I told Joe to do anything he had to keep me away from Ben. I guess that was his way of helping. He's done everything I've asked of him."

"I think you'd be better off sitting down with Ben and hashing it all out. Everything's changed now you know the truth."

"Has it? He still left, Danni. He took the easy way out. What's to say he won't do it again?"

"And what if he won't?"

Glancing over at my best friend as we head towards the airport, I narrow my eyes at how easily she's willing to forgive Ben after everything he put me through. "It doesn't matter, anyway. He thinks I'm with Joe."

Snorting out the coffee she just sipped, she turns her glare on me. "I'm sorry. What? Why?"

"Because we've made it look that way."

"Lauren, please don't tell me you've done what I think you've done," she warns, but the taxi pulls up in front of the airport and cuts off any further conversation. I'm grateful, because I can already tell that Danni's going to give me a serious ear bashing over this. For some reason, she seems to be on Team Ben all of a sudden, and it's pissing me off. Maybe this little trip wasn't such a good idea.

It's not until we're settled on a couple of tall bar stools with a cocktail each that Danni turns her disappointed stare on me.

"Start talking, Lauren." I look around at the happy people surrounding me and let out a sigh. "No point planning your escape. You're not going anywhere."

"Fine. I told Joe that under no circumstances was he to allow me to fall back into any kind of relationship with Ben. He witnessed the majority of the fallout after Ben left the first time, and he was only too happy to agree.

"I didn't think any more of it until Dad's funeral. Ben thought he was hiding in the shadows at the back, but I knew the moment he entered that room. I fought to keep my eyes from seeking him out, but when Joe arrived and pulled me into his arms, I managed to find him. He was staring daggers into Joe's back, and I realised then that the best thing to do to keep him at arm's length was to pretend I was taken."

"And how did that work out for you?" Amusement fills her voice.

"Oh, it was great for all of about six hours, because then I fell into bed with him."

"Lauren, what are you doing?"

"I don't know. That's the problem."

"You're still in love with him, aren't you?"

I look at her over the rim of my glass. She can read me like a book so I don't need to say the words aloud.

"Don't you think you should give him a second chance now you know the truth?" Just remember how good it was. You can always let me know if you don't want him, because I could sure use a little bit of that."

I know Danni's only messing, but still, the thought of her going after Ben has jealousy rising within me. "I'm trying not to think about the good stuff. I'm trying to focus on how much it hurt when he left and reminding myself that I don't ever want to feel that again."

"Lauren," she sighs, realising that she's not getting anywhere. "Hopefully a few days away will help give you some perspective."

"You really think I should forget everything that happened, what he did, and just dive back in?"

"No, I'm not suggesting you continue where you left off at all. I'm suggesting that you at least tell him the truth and spend some time with him...nowhere near a bed, ideally."

"Or a car park," I mutter, but it's not quiet enough.

"You screwed him in a *car park?*"

Groaning, I lift my glass to my lips and drain it. Danni doesn't need the details.

Flight number BA439 to Rome is now boarding. Please make your way to the gate and have your ticket and passport ready.

"READY TO RUN AWAY?" Danni smiles at me innocently, but it's just another way of her showing me how she really feels about what I'm doing with Ben.

"I'm not running. I just need a few days."

"Sure, whatever you say."

"Danni," I breathe, already losing my enthusiasm for this trip.

"No, it's fine. If you say it's what you need, then I'll stop. Let's just go and enjoy ourselves."

A little of my previous excitement flutters in my belly as we finish our drinks and head towards the gate, ready to board our plane.

We've got seats booked, so we don't bother getting up to queue to get on board, instead favouring the uncomfortable seats and enjoying the coffees we stopped to pick up on the walk here.

"I've always wanted to go to Rome," Danni says, pulling out a travel guide. I can't help but groan at her. She's the same wherever we've gone. She's so organised it makes my brain hurt. She's even had an itinerary for the couple of beach holidays we've been on.

"What? I like to know what I'm going to be doing."

"Don't I know it! So what does our schedule look like for the next three days?" I ask with a laugh.

"Well..." She pulls out a list and I burst out laughing.

"You're something else, you know that?"

"You love it."

I sit and listen as Danni talks through our plans and how we're going to squeeze in as much of Rome as humanly possible in the next three days.

Once the queue has died down a little, Danni stuffs her guidebook and list into her bag and we head over.

I feel lighter knowing I'm about to get on a plane and disappear from everything for a few days. What Danni said earlier was wrong: I'm not running away. I'm just going to get my head together, to get some much needed sleep and to hopefully relax—not that I remember seeing that on Danni's schedule. I'm well aware that everything I'm about to leave behind will still be here when I get back. Joe wasn't all that happy about me going at short notice. He tried to convince me to wait until he could get the time off, but I knew I needed to go now. Jenny was equally as disappointed because she believed I should be there for Ben. I know she understood my reasons, and she's trying not to get in the middle of us after warning me about his arrival a few days ago, but she's got her hopes on us sorting everything out. I can

"Lauren, passport," Danni prompts when we're at the front of the queue.

"I'm sorry," I mutter.

I've just taken it and my ticket back when every muscle in my body stills and my stomach turns over.

"Lauren, wait."

"Holy shit. How did he..." Danni trails off as she looks over my shoulder.

His stare burns into my back as Danni's eyes flick between the two of us. I stare at the tunnel just in front of me that's going to take me away from here as my head and heart duel.

"You need to deal with this now, Lauren. Look at him; he should be in a hospital, yet he's here, chasing you down," Danni warns.

I know she's right, but the desire to run right now is so strong. Dragging in a deep breath, I prepare to turn around and see him. I keep my eyes on the floor, afraid of what'll happen if I look at him. I can only imagine the state he's in and how he's managed to get here.

When he was lying in that hospital bed, I prayed that I'd see him up on his feet again, but right now, I hate myself a little for wanting him to be incapable of chasing me.

"Please, don't leave me." My heart hammers against my chest. The attendant next to me gasps, along with a couple of the other passengers waiting to board.

"I'm just going for a few days. I'm not..." I trail off, not really wanting to explain in front of an audience.

"Look at me, Lauren."

My heart continues to pound, and the only sound I can hear is the blood whooshing past my ears. My hands tremble as I fight to keep my eyes from him, but after a few seconds, my need and concern for him gets too much. I drag my eyes up his ripped jeans, over one tattooed arm that's wrapped around his ribs and then the other that's covered in a pristine white cast. His shoulders are slumped, like it's a real effort to keep himself upright. But it's when I get to his face that tears start to burn my eyes and my fingers twitch to reach for him. His usual tanned skin is pale and grey, his eyes are dark, and the bruising down the side of his face is purple and angry.

Our eyes hold and our stare continues for the longest time. I can practically hear his voice begging me to give him a chance to just hear whatever it is he's made all this effort to say.

Eventually, he moves and closes the distance between us. The pain in doing so is clear in his eyes, but I'm frozen to the spot, unable to help in any way.

The stares of the others around us make my skin tingle. We really should be doing this in private, but I'm also aware of what happens the moment we're alone together—although his broken body might be enough to put paid to that right now.

I flinch when his warm palm covers my cheek. He steps right up to me until our foreheads are pressed together.

"Please don't go," he whispers, his eyes pleading with me. "I need you."

His words are like a baseball bat to my chest, and I fight to drag air into my lungs.

"Ben," I breathe, "I can't—"

"You can," he argues. "You can, and you know it. You know this is where you should be." I bite down on my bottom lip, knowing he doesn't mean this country or even this city, but in his arms.

I lose track of time as we stand connected, my body trembling as I try to decide the right thing to do.

This is the final call for passengers travelling to Rome on flight BA439. Please make your way to the gate immediately.

"I'm sorry, but are you getting on the plane?" one of the attendants at the desk asks, dragging my focus away from Ben.

"Uh..."

"You two go. You've got a ticket, right?" Danni asks Ben.

"Yeah," he responds, not taking his eyes from mine. "Up for it?"

Realisation of what Danni's just suggested has me pulling back from Ben to look at her. "But you've planned everything."

"I think you two spending some time together and sorting this shit out is more important than my itinerary, don't you think?"

"I—"

"I'm sorry, but if you're boarding, you really need to move," the attendant presses.

"Come on." Ben threads his fingers through mine

and pulls me towards the tunnel I was so desperate to go down only moments ago.

I look back at Danni, who has a wide smile on her face. "Are you sure?" I ask, hating the idea of leaving her here.

"Of course. You two go. Just promise me you won't spend the whole time arguing and that you'll tell him the truth."

I know her words have Ben turning to look at me. My skin tingles with awareness, but I can't look at him. I daren't.

"Lauren?" he asks, prompting me to move.

"Okay," I say, but I'm not sure if it's for him or Danni. I guess it doesn't really matter because, in seconds, Ben moves and pulls me towards the aeroplane, albeit slowly.

All the other passengers are already seated and ready to go when we make our way up the aisle to find our seats. The two that were reserved for Danni and I are immediately obvious; the flight attendant pointing to them while looking a little harassed isn't necessary.

The doors were shut behind us the moment we boarded, and the second our bums are on the seats she scurries off to start her pre-flight checks. The engines roar and we start backing up. Any chance I had of changing my mind about this are long gone as I sit beside Ben, who has my hand clutched firmly in his.

He's staring at me, and my skin tingles with awareness, but I keep my focus out of the tiny window beside me at the airport we're about to leave. I've no idea if this was a good idea or not. The butterflies in my stomach won't abate, and my heart's still racing.

"You're going to have to acknowledge me at some point, you know?"

"This is insane, Ben," I admit, still keeping my eyes on outside.

"It is. But I also think it's pretty perfect." He leans in, his breath tickling the skin at the base of my neck, and he lowers his voice. "It means I get you all to myself for three whole days." Goosebumps prick my skin and heat floods my core. It's not the reaction I want, but it's no less than I expect when we're in close proximity.

"We're going to spend the time arguing," I state, but my voice comes out all breathy and needy. From the slight catch in his breath, I know he hasn't missed it.

"I could think of worse ways to spend my time. After all, you know what comes after the arguments."

His nose runs around the shell of my ear and my entire body shudders.

"Ben, stop," I beg.

"You're going to need to say it with a little more conviction if you want me to believe you, baby."

"I'm all for talking and hashing everything out properly between us, but that's it. I've already made enough mistakes with you."

"Whatever you say." He chuckles, and his arrogance has me turning to him.

My breath catches once again when I get a look at his bruised face. "I'm deadly serious. Plus, it's not like you'd be able to anyway."

"Trust me, a couple of broken bones wouldn't stop me from giving you what you need."

Christ, this was such a bad idea.

Thankfully, my torture is paused when the flight attendants start doing their safety demonstrations.

I hold my breath once they've finished and wait for what's going to fall from his lips next. But I'm met with silence. When I glance over, I find out why. His head's resting back, and he's fast asleep.

CHAPTER SEVEN

Ben

DANNI'S PARTING words repeat in my mind the whole way to Rome.

Tell him the truth.

I intended on asking her once we were in the air and she had nowhere to hide, but the moment I rested my head back, my exhaustion took over. The effort it took to find her wiped me out. It was only the relief that flooded me when I saw her at the gate that kept me going.

The second she turned and looked into my eyes, I knew I had her. She can tell me as much as she wants that there's no longer anything between us, but it's all lies. She needs to remember that although it's been six years, I know her. I know her like no one else, and I damn well know when she's lying.

"Ben. Ben." Her soft voice and warm hand on my forearm bring me around. "We're about to land."

Blinking a few times, it takes me a couple of seconds to register where I am and what's going on. The last time I woke up I was in a hospital bed, and this time I'm on an aeroplane.

Looking into her kind but tired eyes, something settles inside me. I was on edge from the moment I realised she'd left me in the hospital, but now, with her beside me, I feel right again.

"Thank you." Her brows draw together in confusion. "Thank you for agreeing to this. Thank you for sitting by my bedside and being there when I woke. You've no idea how much that meant to me. I could have done without the ear bashing you gave me moments later, but I can't deny I probably deserved it."

"Of course you did. You hit Joe."

"Uh...no I didn't."

"You did, right before you went down. He's got a black eye to prove it."

Twisting so I can look at her, I cry out as pain

radiates from my ribs. Everyone around us turns to look and I hate the sympathy in their eyes when they take in the state of my face. I've yet to see it properly; I only got a hint of how bad I look in the reflection in the taxi's window.

I suck in a couple of deep breaths before reaching out and taking her hand in mine. She tries to fight me, but I feel so much better when I have some kind of contact with her, so I persist until she gives up.

"Lauren, my memory of what happened is still a little hazy, but I know for a fact that I didn't hit him. I damn well wanted to, but I'm his boss. I can't."

"But—"

"I swear to you, Lauren. I didn't hit him."

"So why would he tell me you did?"

"Because he doesn't want us together."

Lauren sits back, I can almost hear the cogs turning in her head where she's thinking so hard.

"What did Danni mean earlier when she said that you needed to tell me the truth?" Discovering whatever it might be moments before we disembark a plane isn't ideal, but the fact that she's been lying to me is eating at me.

"Not now. Let's get to the hotel, and then we can talk."

I don't want to, but I find myself agreeing

because it's the right thing to do. She obviously doesn't want to talk about it, so I can't imagine having the conversation in front of a few hundred people in a small, enclosed space is the best idea.

"AT LAST," Lauren sighs as she moves towards the luggage belt to grab her case.

"Let me." Leaning forward, I wince in pain and totally miss her bag. Having predicted what was about to happen, Lauren is a few feet in front of me and easily reaches out and lifts it.

"I know you're trying to be all chivalrous, but I've got it," she says with a laugh. I watch as she pulls the little handle out and starts walking towards the exit.

Resting my head back in the taxi, I try to push aside the pain, but the throbbing is starting to get too much. My vision blurs a little, and it's aching all down my face.

"Are you in pain?" Lauren asks, looking over and seeing the tension on my face.

"I'm fine."

"You're lying." Leaning forwards, she asks the driver to stop at a pharmacy on the way to our hotel.

She picks me up the strongest painkillers they

will allow her to buy over the counter. I'm not sure they'll quite cut it, but at this point, anything is better than nothing.

I swallow them down with the bottle of water she also picked up for me, and we continue our journey to the hotel.

"How did you know where to find me?" she asks, looking out the window at the passing city.

"Your emails." Turning back to me, she narrows her eyes in question. "I heard snippets of your conversation planning this trip. I knew whoever you were talking to had sent the confirmations over, so it wasn't all that hard to find out."

An unamused laugh falls from her lips. "I should have known I wouldn't be able to escape you."

"Oh, baby, you've no idea."

The taxi pulls to a stop outside a swanky looking hotel, and I'm reminded that Danni's family business is probably doing better right now than mine is. I really shouldn't be here chasing Lauren halfway around Europe. I should be a home fixing the business like I set out to do before my world came crashing down, quite literally.

"Are you okay? You've gone really pale."

"Yeah, I'm fine." She doesn't look convinced, but she lets it go and gets out of the car.

"Hi, we have a booking under Daniella Abbot." The receptionist clicks about on her computer for a few seconds before agreeing. "I was wondering if it's possible to make it two rooms instead of one?"

"You're shitting me?" The receptionist's eyes widen at my outburst, but she quickly rights herself.

"I'm sorry, Ms Abbot, but we're fully booked."

"Right, okay. Well, thank you for checking."

Lauren reaches out and swipes the key card from the marble counter, collects her things, and marches towards the lift after the woman has given her some brief instructions to find our *one* room.

"Do you need to look so smug?" Lauren asks once we're in the lift.

My lips twitch up at her frustration, and she huffs out another breath.

"Well, that's disappointing, although I reckon we could push them together. What do you think?" I ask when we step inside the room and find two single beds.

"I think they're staying exactly where they are, and you need to stop getting any ideas. Nothing like that is happening. And anyway, you need to rest." She drops her bags down on the first bed. "This one's mine. It's closer to the door in case I need to escape."

I stalk towards her, and she casts her eyes away. I

don't stop until there are only millimetres between us.

"You're not going anywhere, and you know it," I say, breathing in her scent. My fingers twitch to reach out and pull her to me, and my cock swells. "You might tell yourself that you can say no, but we both know you can't. This thing between us…It's too powerful to deny. If it wasn't, we wouldn't be here right now. I wouldn't have been fucking you when you're meant to belong to someone else."

"Fuck you," she spits. Her hands land on my shoulders in an attempt to push me away. Unfortunately, all it achieves is to cause me pain. "Fucking hell. You need to rest."

"Wrong. What I need is you," I admit through gritted teeth as I will the ache in my ribs away.

"Ben, please. Just stop." The fight's left her voice, leaving her sounding tired. "I'm going to go and get us some dinner. You try to make yourself comfortable or something."

"Are you going to be my nurse? I hope you packed your uniform."

Her stare hardens and she slips away from me. "This is going to be a long three days," she mutters as she reaches for her handbag and quickly leaves the room.

Blowing out a long stream of breath, I gently climb on the bed she didn't claim and attempt to get comfortable. What I really need is a shower, but I know I haven't got the strength for that. I might tell Lauren that I'm okay, but it's far from the truth.

I must have drifted off again, because the next thing I know she's walking back through the hotel room door with two giant pizza boxes in her hands. My stomach grumbles right on cue and it reminds me that I've no idea how long ago it was that I actually ate something.

"Hungry?" she asks with a laugh and I delight in seeing a genuine smile on her face.

"Famished." I go to sit up, but every muscle in my body screams for me to stay still.

"Let me help." Rushing over, Lauren puts her hands under my arms and helps me to sit up. She's too tiny to do much, but if it makes her feel like she's helping, then I'm happy. Plus, it means I get her hands on me. It might not be exactly how I want them, but I'll take it. She finds some spare pillows in the wardrobe and uses them to prop me up before placing one of the boxes on my lap.

"That smells incredible."

"You can't beat authentic Italian pizza."

"I guess I'm about to find out."

I moan in ecstasy when I take a bite and the tomato sauce and mozzarella hit my tongue. Lauren's gaze snaps over and her eyes darken as she stares at me.

"Good?"

"So good. Much better than the shitty hospital food I probably would have been served tonight."

"You weren't meant to leave, were you?"

"I wasn't staying."

"That's not an answer."

I shrug and inhale another slice of pizza.

"You'd left, so I had no reason to stay."

"The broken bones weren't enough, huh?"

"Being away from you hurts more."

"Stop, Ben," she sighs.

"I'm only telling the truth."

Guilt floods her features as she realises that I now know she's hiding something from me. "Tomorrow. We'll talk tomorrow."

"Stop putting it off. We should have talked days ago."

"Don't blame all this on me. You're the one who showed up unexpectedly and turned my life upside down."

"I'm not blaming anyone. I just hate this. It should be me and you, baby." I try to fight my yawn, but I can't. Now that I've stopped and the adrenaline of finding Lauren has worn off, I'm exhausted.

"You need to sleep."

I'm too tired to argue, so I allow Lauren to take the empty box from my lap and then help me find a somewhat comfortable position to lie in. I think I fall asleep before my head hits the pillow.

I WAKE with a gentle breeze blowing across my face. Glancing to the side, I find Lauren's bed slept in but empty. The doors at the other side of the room are open, and the light curtains are blowing in the soft wind.

Taking a couple of deep breaths, I prepare to attempt to roll out of bed. The pain hits me like a truck, and any hope I had of it reducing overnight vanishes.

I see her the moment I get to the doors. She's sitting on one of the chairs with her feet propped up on the balcony and her head resting back with her eyes shut. She's bathed in sunlight, and my mouth waters for a taste of her flawless, tanned skin. She's much more breathtaking than the city before us.

I stand there for the longest time, just taking her

in. She's even more beautiful than I remember from all those years ago. Her hair is just as blonde, and her curves are even more sinful than they were back then, but it's her eyes that fascinate me even more now. They hold so much inside them, a wisdom that wasn't there before. It kills me to know it was the pain I caused her that put it there, but I find it sexy as hell nonetheless.

I don't move or make any noise, but somehow she knows I'm here. She looks over her shoulder and her eyes find mine. The intensity in them almost knocks me on my arse.

"So it wasn't a drug-induced dream. I really am in Rome with you."

"So it seems." Her face is serious, but I can see in her eyes that she's at least a little bit happy about it. "How are you feeling?"

"Sore."

"I've got those painkillers in my bag, if you'd like some."

Getting up, she gives me an incredible view of her body wrapped in only a thin, white summer dress. It's cut low enough to give me just a hint of cleavage, and the obvious puckering of her nipples clues me in to the fact that she's not wearing a bra. My mouth waters as I take my time running my eyes over every curve, wishing it were my hands instead.

"Don't get any ideas."

"Oh, baby, I had those years ago. Now I know exactly what I want."

Sidestepping me, she heads back into the room. "Here, take these."

"Thank you."

"I went out first thing and got you some stuff."

Pulling my phone from my pocket, I blanch when I see it's lunchtime. "What did you want to do today? I don't want to ruin your time here."

Shrugging, she drags her eyes away from me. "I didn't come here for the sightseeing, Ben. I just came here to get away."

"You want to go and see stuff though, right?"

"I think it's probably better that you rest."

Nodding, I can't help but agree that a day out wandering around Rome is the last thing I need right now, but if it's what she wants, then I'd do it without question.

"You need to wash. You stink. There's a bath and shower; I don't know what will be easier," she says, pointing to the door at the other end of the room. "I'll be out there if you need me."

She's gone before I get to say anything else, but I

can't argue with what she's saying. I can smell myself, and it's not pleasant.

Walking through to the bathroom, I weigh up my options as I have a pee and use the still packaged toothbrush to freshen my mouth up. I don't want to put too much thought to when the last time I did this was.

Thinking the bath might be my best bet if I want to keep my cast dry, I lower the plug, run the tap and pour in some of the bubbles sat on the side.

I manage to drop my jeans without too much fuss, and I discover that I can slip my socks off without wanting to scream in pain if I sit on the closed toilet seat. Attempting to remove my t-shirt, though, is another matter entirely. After a few minutes fighting, I give up after getting a much better idea. Pulling the door open, I poke my head around the corner. "Lauren, could I get some help?"

It's only seconds before she appears in the doorway. The sight of her in that white dress with the sun shining behind her confirms what a good idea this is. As she walks towards me, I can see every single curve of her body, and my cock swells.

"What's up?"

"I'm struggling. Could you help?" Pulling at the hem of my t-shirt, she drops her eyes.

"You're serious?"

"Deadly. Will you help get me naked?" Raising an eyebrow, she crosses her arms over her chest. "I'm serious. I can't get it off, it hurts too fucking much."

A little sympathy flashes through her eyes, and after letting out a sigh, she follows me into the bathroom, kicking the door shut behind her.

The tension crackles between us the second I turn my stare on her.

"I'm just helping with your shirt, and then I'm going back outside."

Her fingers grasp the fabric and she starts lifting. "Yeah, that's why you shut the door. So you could make a hasty escape."

"It was habit," she argues as I slip my non-broken arm free. Her presence helps to dull the ache in my ribs.

"Yeah, whatever you say, baby."

Lifting up on her tiptoes, she goes to push the fabric over my head. Her breasts brush against my chest, and I can't help my good arm reaching out and wrapping around her waist.

Her movements pause as she sucks in a breath, and when the fabric clears my eyes, I find her staring up at me, desire flooding her features.

I know that if I were to drop my head now, I

could take her lips, but some fucked up part of me is enjoying this game we're playing where she pretends she's not interested. I want to keep it going a little longer; that way, when I do break through the façade she's trying to maintain, it'll be explosive.

"All done." Her voice is a breathy whisper. Her obvious need has my cock almost at full mast.

When she steps back, she takes in the bruising covering my side. Her fingers reach out and she gently touches the purple and green skin. I suck in a breath at her contact.

"Shit, I'm sorry."

"It's okay. It doesn't hurt." It's a small white lie, because it always fucking hurts. My reaction was to the electric shock that shot through my body the moment she touched me. My hand wraps around her wrist to hold her in place, but she quickly tugs it away.

Tucking my thumb into the waistband of my boxers instead, I start pushing them down. I've got no qualms about getting naked in front of her; sadly, she seems to have other ideas.

Turning on her heel, she heads towards the door.

"Ow, fuck," I complain, slightly exaggerating, as I go to sit in the bath.

"Are you okay?" She's back in a flash, holding my

good arm and helping to lower me into the water. I just about manage to keep the smile off my face. She's so easily played.

"Aw, that's good," I moan as the hot water surrounds my aching body. Lauren's cheeks burn red and she looks anywhere but directly at me.

"Are you okay…with the rest?" she asks, awkwardly standing above me.

"It would be easier if you stayed."

Her eyes find mine, and I'm convinced that she's going to tell me where to go and walk out, but to my surprise, she grabs her pink shower puff and a bottle of shower gel and settles herself on her knees beside me.

I watch as she dunks the puff in the water and then squeezes on a generous amount of soap before she gently starts washing across the top of my chest and shoulders.

My head falls back and my eyes close as I revel in the sensation of her taking care of me. She moves lower and very gently brushes my ribs.

"Is that okay?"

"So good," I moan.

Her movements still for a second. "What really happened up on that scaffolding?"

"We were just hashing out some issues."

"Issues?"

"Yeah. He seems to think he's got something that belongs to me." Cracking my eyes open, I glance over at her.

"I don't belong to anyone," she grumbles. "Not him, not you. I'm a person, not a *thing*."

I allow her to vent, because at the end of the day, we both know she's mine. I know for a fact that she's got me in the palm of her hands, and I'll willingly admit that to anyone.

"So there really were no punches thrown?" she asks again, like she didn't believe me the first time.

"No, although it was getting close and I'd have liked nothing better than to knock the smug fucking look off his face as he taunted me."

"Don't," she snaps.

"What? He can't mean all that much to you; I've been inside you twice since I've been back." I know my words are crass, but talking about that fucker riles me up.

"I'm done here," Lauren says, throwing the puff down on my chest, standing and going to storm out.

"Wait. I need you to help me out."

Her shoulders drop as she lets out a giant breath. "Of course you fucking do," she mutters, and I can't help but smile. "Come on then." She stands over me, waiting for me to shift so she can help.

Once I'm sitting, she puts her hands under my arms and does very little to help me, but it's not her help I really want.

I hold back the groan that wants to rumble up my throat as I try to stand, but knowing she's here helps.

"Slowly, Ben," she soothes when I go to step out and catch my toe on the edge of the bath. Her gaze drops, but I'm pretty sure she doesn't make it down to my toes, because my cock is still jutting out in front of me.

Once I'm back on two feet, I reach my good arm out and wrap it around her waist, pulling her up against me.

"Ew, Ben, you're wet."

"I bet you are too," I whisper in her ear. She fights gently to get away, aware that she might hurt me, but I hold tight. "See, you're not even denying it. You know as well as I do that if I were to run my fingers up your thighs, you'd be desperate for me." My cock twitches between us at the thought.

Lauren's eyes darken as she stares up at me, her breathing becoming heavy.

Slowly, I lower my hand. It runs over the curve of her arse until I find the bottom of her dress. My balls ache when my fingers connect with the hot and smooth skin of her legs. I just get to the juncture of her thighs when reality hits her.

"No," she says, jumping back, but she doesn't sound all that convinced.

"Spoilsport." Reaching for a towel, I make a show of rubbing it over my head and across my chest. I make no attempt to cover myself up, because even without looking at her, I can feel her eyes burn into my skin.

"I'm going to look at the room service menu. I'm hungry."

She leaves the room to the sound of my laughter. I'm getting to her, and she knows it. I fully intend on her being mine once again by the time we leave this hotel, and so far it seems to be going exactly as I'd hoped.

The moment she slips from the room, I lean forward against the basin and suck in a few deep breaths. Getting in and out of that bath was much more painful than I tried to let on, and it's still coursing through my body now.

Once everything's eased a little, I wrap a towel around my waist but fail to make it stay put, so I end up holding it.

"Where are you going?" Lauren's standing with

her handbag over her shoulder when I walk out of the bathroom.

"I don't fancy anything on the menu. I saw a little deli down the street so I thought I go and get us some sandwiches."

"Okay, sounds good." Walking past her, I go to the bag she left on the sideboard earlier.

"A-are you going to be okay?" she stutters, a little taken back by my dismissal.

"I'm a fully grown man, Lauren. I think I'll be fine."

She hovers for a few seconds before eventually turning and disappearing.

I don't get a chance to pull out one of the new pairs of boxers she bought for me this morning, because my phone starts ringing on the bedside table. Shuffling over, I pick it up and smile when I see Liv's happy face looking back at me.

"Hello."

"Hey, how's it going up there?"

"I'm in Rome."

"Rome? As in Italy?"

"The one and only."

"What?"

"It's kind of a long story."

"I've got all day."

Walking out to the balcony, I try to sit myself down without groaning in pain, but I'm unsuccessful.

"Are you okay?"

"Yeah, just give me a few seconds."

"Ben, you're worrying me."

Once I've caught my breath, I give Liv the short version of the events of the past thirty-six hours.

"You should be in fucking hospital, not chasing Lauren to Rome."

"All right, Mum."

"I'm serious. You need to look after yourself."

"I'm hoping Lauren's going to do that for me."

"Ugh, you're such a pig."

"It's part of the reason why you love me."

"Hmm…yeah," she mumbles.

"Is everything okay down there? I miss the beach."

"Everything's pretty much as it always is, just without you. You should bring Lauren to visit."

"I intend to. If I ever make her see sense."

"That's kind of why I'm ringing."

"To make Lauren see sense?"

"No. Yes. Kind of."

"You're going to need to give me a little more than that, Liv."

"Okay, well, I've been looking into stuff, and I've found something you might find interesting."

"Go on."

"I'm going to send you some pictures over."

I pull the phone from my ear, put Liv on speaker and wait for her messages.

My phone vibrates and I open the first picture. It's a photo of a newspaper article about locals helping out to fix their community centre roof. Frowning, I zoom in and suddenly it makes sense. *Image above: Nick Davis and Joseph Kingsman* (*aged 6*) *after donating their time to fix the roof*.

Nick knew Joe prior to him being friends with Lauren? Questions start spinning around in my head as my phone buzzes again.

"I just thought that was interesting, but it's the next one you really need to see. Ready?"

The three little dots bounce and my impatience grows as I wait to see what's coming next.

It's fuzzy when it first comes through, and it takes a while to load, but when it does, my eyes widen and my chin drops. "Holy fucking shit."

CHAPTER EIGHT

Lauren

I TOLD myself when I agreed to this trip with him that I wouldn't do anything stupid. I've already made enough bad decisions when it comes to Ben to last a lifetime. But then I find myself arm-deep in his bath water, gently cleaning his broken and bruised body. I know he wants me; the evidence was pointing directly at me when I helped him step into the tub. I need to get my head together. We need to talk and find a way for us to continue to be around each other if he stays, which seems likely now he's taken over the business.

I'm not all that hungry after making the most of the continental breakfast the hotel had to offer this morning while Ben was still fast asleep, but it's the only excuse I can think of to get me out of that tiny hotel room and away from him before I do something I'm going to regret. He's not happy about it—he made that obvious when he appeared with bubbles and water droplets still running down his sculpted body and a towel barely covering his still erect cock. One glance at it and I knew I needed at least a few minutes break; it was calling to me like a fucking ice-lolly.

The second I step foot outside the room, I feel like I can breathe once again. I spend the short walk trying to come up with how I'm going to explain everything properly to him. Thanks to Danni dropping me in it yesterday, desperation to know the truth pours from his eyes every time I look at him. I'm amazed he's allowed me this long without demanding to know what I'm hiding, but I know that's soon to come to an end, and it's got to be better coming from me willingly than him having to drag it out of me, right?

I can't be gone any longer than twenty minutes, but as I walk towards our hotel room door my nerves get the better of me. Sucking in a few deep breaths, I prepare to tell him something that could change everything for us. Depending on how he takes it, I'm not sure if I'm going to be able to hold back. I know I should be stronger, should stand up for what I believe is right, but this is Ben I'm talking about. I've never been able to let my head lead the way where he's concerned.

The room's silent and deserted when I walk in. Dropping my handbag on my bed, I continue towards the open French doors with the bag from the deli in my hand. I find Ben sitting in the chair I was in earlier, staring down at his phone. He'd have heard the door shutting, so he knows I'm here, but he's yet to turn to me and that has the nerves that are fluttering in my belly exploding.

Something's wrong.

Eventually, he lowers his phone and slowly turns his face my way. Anger pulls at his features, his eyes hard with accusation.

"W-what is it?"

"I think you need to start explaining, don't you?"

"Shaking my head, I try to figure out what he's talking about, but I've no idea what could have possibly happened in the short time I was gone.

"I've no i-idea what—"

"Don't talk shit. You know exactly what I'm

talking about. *Danni* knows exactly what I'm talking about. She already warned me."

My stomach drops and my hands tremble. I guess me wanting to get in there first has been shot to shit.

"I suggest you sit down."

"I...I'm good."

"Sit," he barks, and my body does as it's told.

"You remember Liv?" I nod briefly. She was the one who came over before I even knew who she was and told me that Ben still loved me. I kind of wanted to punch her in the face at the time, but I know she was only trying to help.

"Yeah."

"Did you know she's a journalist?" I shake my head, my heart racing. "Well, she is. And do you know what journalists are good at?" Shaking my head again, I wait for him to say the inevitable. "Would you like to be honest, or do I need to drag it out of you?"

Tears burn my eyes as he stares daggers at me. I knew he'd be angry if—when—he found out, but I didn't quite appreciate the level of anger I'm looking at right now.

"Joe and I..." I trail off, not really knowing how to put it.

"Yeah...?"

"We're not together," I admit, looking down at where my fingers are playing with the hem of my dress.

"Good. And why not?"

"Because he's...not interested in me," I whisper, feeling the weight of the lie I told pressing down on me.

"Now, that wasn't that hard was it?" he spits. I sniff as my emotions start to get the better of me, but his stare doesn't waver. "I fucked you, thinking we were betraying another man. You allowed me to believe that what we were doing was wrong. But the whole fucking time, you were mine to take."

"I'm sorry, I—"

"What?" he snaps.

"I thought it would keep you away." The laugh that falls from his mouth has a shiver running down my spine.

"Keep me away? Fucking hell, Lauren. You should know that nothing would have kept me away."

"But it did," I scream. "My dad kept you away for six fucking years. Six fucking years, Ben. You just disappeared and I had no fucking idea what to think. I had no choice but to get on with my life, and Joe was like a breath of fresh air when I met him. He listened to me in a way no one else did. He understood in a way that no one else could, and by some miracle he brought me back to life."

"He threatened me, Lauren. Threatened you. If I didn't leave, he was going to take everything from both of you. I did what I thought was the best thing for you at the time. I was young, naïve, and I thought I was doing you a favour. I don't give a fuck about Joe, Lauren. You lied to me." He stands, and I hate the feeling of him looking down on me like I could be less than him.

"You left me," I fume, standing, holding his stare. "I risked everything for you and you fucking left."

His jaw tenses, the muscles in his neck pulsing with anger, his increased breaths rushing over my face. Then I blink, and everything changes.

His fingers tangle in my hair and I'm pulled against his mouth. His tongue parts my lips and I accept him inside willingly. Our tongues tangle and duel as we pour our anger and frustrations into our kiss. Teeth clash and bite, but it only spurs me on. I step up to him, but his casted arm stops me from pressing myself against him and feeling the hardness of his muscles against me.

Reaching my hands around his back, I run my nails down until I hit the waistband of his boxers. A growl rumbles up his throat, sending my desire into overdrive. Slipping my hands into his underwear, I grab onto his arse and start walking him backwards into our room. I should be putting a stop to this. I told myself I wouldn't allow this to happen, but with his lips on mine and his hand on me, I'm powerless to do anything but to give in to what my body craves. And right now, it wants what Ben can give me more than it wants air.

"I fucking need you, Lauren," he moans when he comes to a stop by his bed and rips his lips away from mine.

Dropping his face to my neck, he starts pulling at the strap over my shoulder with his one working arm, but it doesn't get him very far.

To help him out, I turn so he can find the zip. Pulling my hair to the side, I give him access to my bare skin. He wastes no time in dropping his lips to me, kissing and licking his way towards the fabric. Once he's there, he finds the zip and slowly drags it down. The sensation of the fabric tickling my skin has lust shooting to my core. I moan as it falls from my shoulders, catching on my peaked nipples.

Ben sucks in a breath as he steps back and takes in my bare skin. "I'll never get enough of you, baby." Turning me, he pushes me down on the bed and encourages me to lie back when he places his knee beside me. Pain twists his face and it's obvious that he's not able to take charge right now like he'd like to.

Slipping out from under him, I place my hands gently on his waist and push him towards the bed. His eyes widen as he stares down at me.

"Just do as you're told." His expression darkens. His eyes flick over my face before dropping down to my bare breasts.

"I think I can manage that."

Tucking my thumbs into the sides of my thong, I make a show of pushing it from my hips. Ben's cock twitches behind the fabric of his boxers, and it's all the encouragement I need. "Tell me if it hurts too much."

"Never." I give him a hard stare, but he doesn't waver.

"Lie back and take what I've got to give you."

"My pleasure." He slowly drops his back to the bed, his eyes never leaving me.

My heart hammers in my chest and my core throbs for what's to come.

Once he's settled, I grab onto the elastic of his boxers and pull them down his legs. His cock springs back against his stomach and my mouth waters. But as much as I may want to taste him right now, I'm too impatient for what I need. I need something to break the tension within, and Ben is the only way I know how.

Climbing up his body, I try not to move the mattress too much, but he still winces in pain. I know I should stop. There are a million reasons why I should, but I already know that none of them are enough to stop me right now.

I take him in my hand once I'm hovering over his waist. His body tenses with the sensation, and his eyelids flutter in pleasure. Lining myself up with him, I slowly sink down, gasping when he fills me to the point I swear I might burst.

"Fuck," I moan when my body gets exactly what it needs.

Dragging my eyes open, I stare down at Ben. Both pain and pleasure are etched onto his handsome face. His eyes are hard with anger still, and his teeth grind, making his jaw pop. He needs this release just as much as me.

Lifting up, I drop down on him, probably harder than I should, and we both cry out. But I don't stop. I pour every bit of anger, regret and remorse for what we both lost and what we could have been into my movements as I fuck him with everything I have. He lies lifeless below me, his fist clutching the sheets beneath him. I've no idea if it's because of pleasure or pain. A sadistic part of me hopes it's the latter, punishment for everything he put me through since the day he walked out of my life and now everything he's dragged back up since reappearing.

"Fuck, shit," I moan as my release starts to creep up on me. I can only feel the beginning tingles, but I know it's going to knock me for six. A few minutes of mind-numbing pleasure to forget is exactly what I need right now.

Grinding my hips down on him, I take everything I need to push myself over the edge.

"Shit, Lauren. Fuck, baby," he groans. The muscles in his neck are pulled tight, his eyes squeezed shut. I know he's getting close, I can feel him swelling within me.

I drop down on him one more time, and my body takes over as my orgasm slams into me. Light flashes behind my eyes as heat radiates through my body. My muscles convulse and I have to fight my need to collapse onto his body beneath me as I drag in lungfuls of air.

"Oh, shit."

He's just about to come; I know his tells like the back of my fucking hand. In a moment of madness—

or weakness—I pull myself off him and climb off the bed.

"W-what? Lauren, what the—" Ben stutters as his body realises what's just happened. He cries out in pain as he tries to sit up to find out what's going on. By the time he opens his eyes, I've got my dress up my body and my bag and flip-flops in my hand.

Turning to look over my shoulder, I take in the panic on Ben's face. "Not a nice feeling, is it?" I pause for one second before marching from the room.

My heart pounds as the hotel room door slams shut behind me.

"Lauren," Ben roars and my stomach turns over.

What the fuck did I just do?

I quickly zip up my dress and drop my flip-flops to the floor so I can slide them on. Ben continues shouting before there's a loud bang and a cry sounds out. I instinctively turn and reach for the door handle, but at the last second, I change my mind and walk away.

CHAPTER NINE

Ben

"FUUUUCK," I groan as the pain radiating from my ribs renders the rest of my body useless. In my need to get to her, I misjudge the width of the mattress and end up on the fucking tiled floor. My ribs scream in pain and my arm aches where I landed on the fucking cast.

"Lauren," I shout once again, but I know it's already too late. She's gone. Gone fuck only knows where in a foreign fucking city.

It takes me longer than I want to admit to get up off the floor, but I eventually manage to drag my aching, tense body back out to the balcony to find my phone. When I unlock it, the photo of Joe hovering over another man's lips lights up on my phone, and another wave of anger washes through me. She was fucking lying to me this whole time. Part of me knew something wasn't right. The warning signs have been there the whole time. He knew we'd slept together yet he didn't lay a finger on me. If someone else so much as looks at her the wrong way when she's mine, I'll break their fucking nose, so the fact he hardly even flinched should have been evidence enough. But the image of them both standing in their doorway looking all loved up when she sent me away still haunts me. They were so convincing. My fist clenches with my need to do something, to break something...or someone. I knew I should have fucking hit him on that scaffolding.

Finding Lauren's number, I lift my phone to my ear. It takes forever to connect, but when it does, it goes straight to voicemail.

"Fucking hell." Throwing it down on the table, I rest my head back and squeeze my eyes shut. My entire body is strung tight, desperate for the release that was so fucking close. My cock twitches at the memory of being inside of her and how tight she squeezed me as she got herself off. Lifting my head, I gaze down at my useless right arm. I might be right on the edge, but I already know that my left hand won't cut it.

I knew she was angry. Her eyes had pure hatred oozing from them as she climbed on top of me, but I'd no idea she was planning on leaving me high and dry.

Over the next few hours, I continue trying her phone, but at no point does it even ring. I've just about lost my fucking mind by the time I hear the click of the key card in the lock later that evening—hours after she walked out.

Moving as quickly as I can, I'm in the doorway when she comes into view. It takes her a few seconds to lift her eyes from the floor, but when she does, all I see is hurt.

"Fuck." Pushing my own pain aside, I walk up to her and pull her into me. The second she's in my arms, her body trembles and her cries take over. A lump forms in my throat and my eyes sting as my own tears threaten.

"I'm sorry," I whisper into her hair as the reality of how much we're hurting each other hits me. "I'm so sorry."

We cling onto each other for the longest time, but eventually her breathing evens out and her trembling subsides. She pulls back to look at me, her blue eyes swimming behind unshed tears.

"Where the hell have you been?" It comes out harsher than I intended, and her body stiffens before she forces herself from my arms.

"Where have I been?" she repeats, as if it's the most insane question she's ever been asked. "How fucking dare you." My eyes widen, taken back by her sudden anger. "I was gone for a few hours, and you were worried sick. How the fuck did you think I felt when you left for six fucking years, Ben?"

"I—" I swallow the emotion bubbling up my throat. She's right.

She blows out a long breath and I see her fight leave her. Her eyes drop from mine to where I'm holding my ribs. "Are you okay after…"

"After you fucked me half to death? Yeah, I'm good."

Her cheeks blush and she looks away. "Liar." She gives me a weak smile and I can't really argue because my ribs hurt like a motherfucker. "I picked you up some more painkillers. Here." She hands me a bag and heads out to the balcony. "We need to talk," she says, sensing me behind her. She's resting her palms on the railings, looking out at the ancient city in the distance. "We need to talk without shouting or fucking. We need to find a way to move past this... bullshit. I'm exhausted, Ben, and you've only been back a few days. We can't keep rehashing the same shit over and over."

"Here." At the sound of my voice, she turns and takes the bottle of water in my outstretched hand.

"Thank you." Our fingers touch as she takes it, and our eyes connect. There's no denying that the connection we had all those years ago is still there. If anything, it's stronger now. I know what I want to do about it; I've just no idea if Lauren's willing to give me the second chance I want. I know it's what she wants. I can see it in her eyes every time she looks at me. The question is, will she allow herself to go there again?

She watches as I carefully lower myself to the chair I've been sitting in, waiting for her to return. I wince in pain and she flinches like she can feel it too.

"We shouldn't have done that earlier. You need to be resting, healing."

"I'll never say no to you, Lauren. You should know that by now."

"Enough," she snaps, and my eyes fly to hers. "We're not doing this. We're just talking."

"You were the one who brought it up," I sulk, a

smile playing at my lips. Thankfully, she takes it the way I intended and her lips twitch too.

"Ben...I—" She twists her hands in front of her.

"Hey, it's okay. Whatever it is, you can tell me." Taking her hand in mine, I squeeze gently, hoping to give her the strength she needs to talk.

"It's not that. It's just...revisiting that time is painful."

"I know, baby. I'm so, so—"

"No more apologies, okay? Let's forget all the blame and who did what and just talk." Nodding, she takes a few seconds to collect her thoughts. "Joe was...my guardian angel. He turned up looking for a job, and I found a best friend. I was drowning. You leaving like that...it fucking broke me, Ben. I can't even describe how I felt that morning or in the days and weeks that followed. I was like this hollow shell of a person just drifting between work and home, but not really being in either place. My head and my heart were stuck in my memories of us. It was the only way I could get up every morning and function. Dad played the perfect doting father. My first reaction was to accuse him for your disappearance, but he did such a good job of acting like he was concerned and trying to support me that I believed every fucking lie that fell from his lips. He picked out every tiny one of your flaws and used it to show me how untrustworthy you were, how you were never the kind of guy you pretended to be. Without you there, everything he was saying just made sense. I knew my dad wasn't perfect or even that good a human being, but I really never thought he'd have a hand in something that would cause me so much pain. So the naïve child that I was took everything he said as gospel.

"I honestly didn't think I'd see daylight the same as I once did ever again. My world was black, and there didn't seem to be a way out. I almost bailed on my place at uni, and I stopped turning up to work. Your mum tried to do what she could, but every time I looked at her, all I could see was you. It took me a long time to be able to form the kind of relationship we have now, despite the effort she put in. She was the only one who had some kind of understanding of how I felt. She came and laid with me in the dark in my room one night and told me all about your dad. She sobbed the whole way through, as if just telling the story felt like she was losing him all over again. Our relationship changed after that. We'd found some kind of common ground, and we were able to start again.

"It wasn't until Joe turned up that things started

to change. To be honest, I thought Dad was going to take one look at him, see the similarities to you and send him back out where he came from. But he must have seen something in him, because he offered him a job labouring. Erica dragged us all out on her compulsory first day on the job drinks outing, and we became fast friends. He was having issues with his parents—they'd kicked him out and cut him off. We just kind of clicked. He understood what I was going through, and he just knew the right thing to say."

My stomach knots as I get a front row seat to the pain I caused her six years ago. I can see the shadows lingering in her eyes as she explains it. I'm desperate to make it all go away, to remind her of the good stuff and how incredible we are when we're together, but I know talking about this stuff has to happen. We can't put it off by arguing or fucking any longer.

"I think everyone expected us to get together. We were spending more and more time together, but there was always something missing for that to be possible. I love Joe, he means so much to me, but not once has there been anything more than friendship between us. It took him quite a long time to open up to me about his sexuality. It was ultimately what led to the breakdown of his relationship with his parents."

"With him in my life, I felt like I could actually move on. Uni was…fine. I made the best of it. Work was also okay. I loved working with Erica and Joe, and Dad was as overbearing as ever, but we all made it work. I even went on a few dates." My entire body tenses with her admission. "What?" she asks with a laugh. "You thought I'd been celibate all this time in the hope you'd come back?"

"I…uh…" Just the thought of her being with other men has my muscles tensing, ready to fight.

"Have you been? Celibate?"

An unamused laugh falls from my lips as the faces of the women I've spent time with over the past six years fill my mind. "Something like that," I mutter eventually.

"I'll take that as a no then. None of that matters though. I never met anyone who I could imagine spending more than one night with, let alone the rest of my life. You ruined me, Ben. No one else stood a chance after you."

My heart swells at her honesty. Leaning forward, I thread our fingers together, revelling in the feeling of her smooth skin against mine once again.

"I hadn't planned to use Joe to lie to you, but all of a sudden here you were, and I panicked. He knew everything about us, and I'd already told him numerous times over the years that, if you were ever to turn up again, he was to do anything in his power to stop me falling back into bed with you." My eyebrow rises in amusement; she knew that even after six years she wouldn't be able to resist me even before I turned back up. "You can wipe that smug look from your face," she warns, but she's fighting a smile.

"I thought that by pretending we were a couple, you might back off. I clearly didn't think it through properly."

"I think you underestimated me. Or us. Everyone else backed you up. I assume they all know you're not a couple."

Guilt twists her features. "I asked them all to play along. They weren't happy. Erica and your mum especially."

"I guess I should be slightly pleased that they weren't totally on board with the plan," I say sadly, thinking how quick everyone was to lie to me.

"You need to remember that it wasn't just me you hurt by leaving. Your mum and Erica were devastated too, and they had to watch me crumble. You shouldn't really be surprised that they were willing to back me up."

"I'm not." Although what she's saying hurts, I

know it's true. I hurt a lot of people by disappearing like I did, a lot more than I intended to.

"Dad's death came out of the blue. He seemed fine in the days before he died. I had enough on my plate looking after your mum and knowing that someone was going to have to take over the business; I knew I wouldn't be able to cope. The last thing I expected the day I turned back up at work was to find you there, staring at me as if six years hadn't passed. I'd fought every day since you left to put you behind me, and there you were. I just...I didn't..."

Moving my chair closer, I put my arm around her shoulder. "It's okay. I didn't expect you to be there, either. Chris had asked me to get some paperwork and told me that you'd not been to the office since Nick had passed. I thought it was safe. I thought I had time to prepare for seeing you. I soon realised that nothing I did could have prepared me for that."

She looks up at me through watery eyes, and my heart aches for her, for everything I've put her through.

CHAPTER TEN

Lauren

IT FEELS good to finally tell Ben how it really felt when he left instead of just shouting at him. Being able to see his reaction reminds me that I'm not alone in this. I've been carrying around this anger and bitterness for so long that it's hard to accept that he's always felt the same. I'd no idea that when I was trying to get someone to understand how I felt, that the one person I'd swore I never wanted to see again was the only one who would truly get it. The longer I talk, the more I realise that my anger's been directed at the wrong person since finding out the truth. Yes,

Ben was the one who walked out that night, but it wasn't of his own doing. And while I may always wonder what might have happened if he'd stayed and fought for us, I do understand why he thought he was doing the best thing. It might have been a little naïve and misguided, but his young heart was in the right place.

As he thinks back to the day he walked back into the office, pain and regret fill his eyes. "I'd convinced myself over the years that you'd hate me. It was no less than I deserved. But I knew your dad wouldn't have let me off lightly. I knew I was going to be the bad guy; he wasn't likely to admit his part in it. I told myself that you'd have moved on, found someone else. That you'd be happy. Then you glanced up from your desk and you looked at me exactly how I remember, and I knew. Nothing had really changed. I knew you were still mine."

I blow out a long breath as the realisation that he can read me so well after all this time settles within me. How is it possible that after six years, nothing can really change?

"Tell me about your life. What did you do when you left?"

"I got on the first train I found and ended up in Exeter. I was about as lost as you described earlier. I found a crappy bedsit and pretty much drank myself into oblivion for quite a long time.

"Then one day I saw an advert saying something about it not being too late to apply to university, and I thought why not. I had absolutely nothing else to fill my time with."

"You got a degree?"

"Yeah, you don't need to look so shocked. I'm actually kinda smart."

"I know you are. I just never imagined you studying."

"Me either," he admits. "But I had no idea what to do. I'd just walked away from everything that was important to me. I signed up to a business course, I still had hope then that it might come in useful if I ever got the chance to take over Johnson & Son's like I always planned to. I met Dec on the first day. We hit it off instantly and went out for drinks straight from our first lecture. He asked me about home and family, and I panicked. I put on this act from that very first day, and it became second nature."

"An act?" My brows draw together.

"I didn't want him or anyone digging into why I was there. I could barely think about it, let alone talk about you and the reason I had to leave, so I covered it up. I covered it by becoming the kind of guy I hoped the others would look up to. Who would appear so confident that they'd never need to ask about my past, because there's no way I could have any secrets hidden in my closet."

"I'm not sure I understand."

He blows out a breath and casts his eyes away. "I played up to my new nickname with alcohol and..." His face twists as if it's painful to admit.

"And?"

"Women."

My stomach drops. I knew there was no way he hadn't been with anyone else, but hearing him say it makes me feel a little sick.

The word seems to echo forever in the silent space around us. I want to ask more questions, find out more about what he did when we were apart, but my head's full of unwanted images of him with faceless women, treating them the way he does me.

"I'm sorry," I say in a rush and run to the bathroom, afraid I'm about to lose the contents of my stomach.

Slamming the door behind me, I come to a stop in front of the basin, rest my palms on the marble top and hang my head. I drag in a few deep breaths, hoping it'll help settle my stomach. My eyes burn, but I refuse to cry. What he did was perfectly acceptable given the circumstances. Plenty of people said I should have been doing the same thing, but I could never switch him off enough to really go through with it.

I'm surprised when he doesn't immediately chase me, but I'm grateful that he allows me a few seconds to process what he said and to attempt to deal with it in private. That said, it can't be five minutes later when a knock sounds on the door.

"Lauren, are you okay?"

"Yeah, I'm fine. I'll be out in a few seconds." My voice sounds pathetic, making me wish I were stronger.

As I stare at my pale face in the mirror, the movement of the door handle catches my attention. In a second, it's open and Ben's in the doorway, staring at my reflection.

"None of them ever meant anything. None of them ever managed to make me forget you for even a second. It's only ever been you, baby."

The tears I was fighting so desperately hard to keep in drop onto my cheeks. The sincerity on his face doesn't falter as he says the words, and I believe every single one of them.

Turning on my heels, I run at him.

"Fuck," he grunts the second I collide with his

body, and I immediately feel awful for not being more careful.

"I'm sorry, I'm sorry," I repeat, trying to pull away but he only holds onto me tighter. He must be in agony, but he doesn't loosen his grip until I stop fighting.

Running his hand up my back, he slips it into my hair and gently pulls so I have no choice but to look up at him. "Only ever you," he whispers before dropping his lips to mine for the sweetest kiss I think I've ever received. It's like my whole body sighs as his lips brush over mine. It's the first kiss we've shared since he's been back that isn't fuelled by anger and frustration. I wish it could go on forever. But as my body's gearing up for more, he pulls back. My head knows it's the right thing to do. The last thing I need is to fall back under his spell. His eyes are dark and full of emotion when he stares down at me. I can tell he wants to say more, but he's holding himself back. It's not the first time he's tried to open up about how he feels about me since reappearing, but I think it's the first time I'd be able to accept the words if he were to say them.

"Do you fancy getting out of this hotel room? I could really do with dinner."

"That sounds perfect. Let me just freshen up a little, and I'll help you get dressed."

WE WALK OUT of the hotel room hand in hand, and it's almost easy to believe that we're just a normal couple enjoying a few days away from the pressures of everyday life. But one look to my left to see his cast and bruised face and I realise once again that we're far from that.

We might have had a bit of a breakthrough in the last few hours, but we've still got a long way to go if we have any hope of a future, whether that's together or just as...family. I screw my nose up at the thought. Are we still even really that now? Dad's gone. Jenny will hopefully move on and find the happiness she deserves. Where does that leave us?

He must feel a change in me, because he looks over, his own eyes seeming brighter than they have in the last few days.

"You okay?"

"Yeah. I'm good, I think. How are you holding up?" He tried to put on a brave face as I helped him dress, but I could see the pain etched into his face every time he moved.

"I'll survive."

"Right, what do you fancy?" I ask when we step foot outside the hotel.

"You."

"I meant for dinner. I was thinking Italian," I say with a laugh. It feels so good not to be constantly arguing with him.

"Italian sounds perfect."

We've barely started our main, and Ben's already fighting back his exhaustion. It was easy to forget what he went through only days ago as we hashed out everything else, but he really needs to rest. I insisted on stopping at the first restaurant we found when it became obvious that navigating the cobblestones was causing him pain.

"Tell me about Devon," I say, hoping to perk him up a little. "You mentioned that you lived by the sea."

"Dec bought this old derelict house after we graduated. The place was a serious shithole, but he had a dream. He was originally going to tidy it up and pay to get it renovated as and when he could afford it. He was starting a new surfing business at the time, so money was tight. Then one night when I'd had a little too much to drink, I let slip that I knew my way around a building site and offered to help. I didn't need a paying job, thanks to..." He trails off, but from the look on his face, he doesn't need to say more. "With the help of a few local tradesmen, we did the entire place. It's incredible. It looks right out onto the sea. You'd love it."

"I'd love to go one day."

He looks up with a forkful of pasta halfway to his mouth. "You really want to?"

"Of course. I want to see where you were living, what you were doing. I'd also like to meet your friends properly. Things were a little...stressed when they came to visit."

He studies me for the longest time. "Wha—" He clears his throat, anxious about what he wants to say to me. "What are we doing here?"

Thoughts of the future and trusting him again have my heart rate increasing, but a future without him in it would be even more panic attack inducing.

"We're just taking things one day at a time." I don't know how else to get across how I'm feeling. After all these years, he still means so much to me, but I'm terrified of being hurt again.

Nodding, he takes a sip of his water. "That sounds perfect."

It's nice to spend a few hours like a normal couple—not that we're either normal or a couple. But memories from the last time we were in a restaurant together aren't far from my mind. That night had promises of being incredible, but instead it was the beginning of the end.

"Stop thinking about it," he warns.

"How'd you know?"

"I can read you like a book. Plus, I was thinking the same thing. It's going to be different this time, baby. Just give us a chance." Stretching his hand across the table, he tangles our fingers together, rubbing my palm with his thumb.

The lump in my throat grows too big to be able to talk.

"What's wrong?"

"N-nothing," I stutter. "Just thinking about that night." It's an excuse, and I think he knows it but I'm not ready to put all my fears out on the table quite yet. Today has been draining enough already.

"Are you done?"

"Yeah. Let's get out of here. You need to rest."

"Rest wasn't exactly what I had in mind."

"That's a real shame, Ben, because that's all you're getting." I can't help but laugh as he sticks his bottom lip out in a childish pout. "One day at a time, remember?"

"If you say so," he mutters, gently tucking me against his side as we make our way back to the hotel.

I want to relax into it like he wants me too, but I'm not ready to put all my trust in him again. He's going to have to fight for it.

The closer we get to the hotel, the slower he becomes, and it's just the reminder we both need that the only thing that's happening once we get inside the room is him sleeping. What started out as him holding me soon turns into me helping him along the corridor to our room.

"We're almost there."

"This is fucking ridiculous. I've hardly done anything all day."

"You're broken, Ben. It's going to take some time."

"Argh, fuck," he groans, lifting his arms so I can pull his t-shirt from his body. "I haven't got time. I've got things I want to do now." Dropping his head to my neck, his lips tickle against my sensitive skin.

"Not happening," I warn.

"Try saying that when you're not undoing my trousers." A laugh rumbles up his throat and the sound has butterflies erupting in my stomach.

"I meant what I said earlier. One day at a time. That means everything, Ben. I'm not ready to pick up where we left off like six years hasn't passed. So much has changed. We've both changed. We need time to get to know each other again. We might be totally incompatible now."

"You're kidding, right?" As he gently lowers himself to the bed, my eyes lose their fight and run down the length of him. Dark tattoos cover his arms and chest. His stomach is more defined than I remember it being, and my mouth waters to discover the ridges more intimately. Running my eyes down over the elastic of his boxers, I find the evidence of what me undressing him really did to him.

"It's been like that since you upped and left earlier. Fancy finishing the job?"

His eyes are dark and his jaw clenches with need. My mouth waters as the idea of giving him what he needs pops into my head, but it goes against everything I just told him I wanted.

When I glance back up, his eyes are half-closed, and it's not with desire. It's the reminder I need. Him in touching distance is too bloody tempting. It would be too easy to pretend that I'm a careless eighteen-year-old again. If we're going to do this properly and have any chance of rekindling what we had, then I truly believe taking things slowly is the way forward. Pulling the sheets from the bottom of the bed, I cover his body.

"I'm going to go and change. I'll be back in a few minutes. Shout if you need anything."

"Lauren," he calls, just before I disappear into the bathroom.

"Yeah?"

When I turn back, his eyes are closed, although the tension in his body means he's anything but relaxed.

"I never stopped loving you. I need you to know that."

"I know," I whisper.

CHAPTER ELEVEN

Ben

I FELT a little more like myself the next day, so Lauren and I spent a couple of hours in the city. We had a very slow walk around the Colosseum and threw coins in the Trevi Fountain. I tried to put on a brave face, but Lauren could tell I was struggling. The moment she spotted a sightseeing bus, she bought us both tickets and we enjoyed the rest of the city from the open top. I hoped she was trying to reserve my energy for when we got back to the hotel room, but I was bitterly disappointed when I once again fell asleep in my tiny single bed with her in her own only a few feet away.

I'm not sure if she's trying to torture me on purpose, but my balls are bluer than I thought possible after she walked out mid-sex the previous day. She's standing by her words and not taking things too far. I've no idea how long she intends to continue it; every time I ask, she just repeats the same words about taking each day as it comes.

Our alone time passes us by all too quickly, and before I know it, we're back at the airport, preparing to head back to whatever our lives might hold.

"Are you ready to head back and take the building world by storm?" she asks with a laugh, dragging her eyes away from the little aeroplane window beside her.

"No."

"It is what you want, though?"

"Right now, all I want is you. My wanking hand's in a cast, and you're all the way over here." Running my nose around the shell of her ear, her body shudders before she gently pushes me away.

"Behave," she warns, raising an eyebrow, prompting me to answer her original question.

"Honestly, taking over that business is the only thing I've ever wanted to do. But..."

"But?"

I sigh. "I never imagined it would be quite like this." A sad smile tugs at her lips.

"I feel like all of this is my fault." It's the first time she's said anything about work the whole trip. "I should have seen that something was wrong. I manage the accounts, for fuck's sake. I had no idea there was no money."

"Don't even think of shouldering the guilt for him, Lauren. Your dad was a scumbag, and he made sure he covered his tracks so you wouldn't find out." She visibly pales at hearing those harsh words, but they're true, and she's going to have to find a way to deal with it.

"I still should have known. How bad is it?"

"Bad. We're going to have to let people go. Mum suggested we look at moving offices to somewhere cheaper but—"

"That's where your dad chose for the business." Looking over, I reach out and take her hand in mine. She's always had this ability to know exactly what I'm thinking, what I'm feeling, and this is no exception.

"Yeah. I know it's the most sensible thing to do, but I can't help feeling like I'm betraying him."

"He would understand, Ben. He would want you

to do whatever it takes to save the company, and if that means we run it from the double garage at Jenny's, then that's what we'll do."

"We?" I ask, my voice filled with hope. Her expression drops as she thinks over what she said.

"Oh...uh. I don't—"

"Just come back, please?"

"I don't think it's a good idea." I study her face for any sign she's lying, but I don't see anything.

"But we need you."

"No, you don't," she says sadly. "Erica's more than capable. You won't even notice I'm not there."

"Don't. You belong there just as much as I do."

"No, I don't. I was only there because of him. Everyone's going to think I was involved or whatever." She tries brushing the conversation off with a flick of her hand, turning back to the window and trying to cut me off.

"Lauren, I want you there with me."

"No," she barks, and I have no choice but to drop it—for now, at least.

"Have you spoken to Erica?" She shakes her head. "I think you should."

"You seem to have a lot of opinions on what I should do for someone who hardly knows me." Her words cut, but I can't really argue. I do feel like I've just been slapped with her change of attitude, mind you. "I'm sorry," she whispers. "I just...ugh. All this shit just happened all at once. I need to process one thing at a time, and you might be surprised to hear that *you* were more persistent."

"I don't know what you mean. Has she tried to talk to you?"

"Yeah. She's been texting me for days, but I just... she was sleeping with him, Ben"

"I know, but I really think you should hear her out. She said she was in a bad place after her ex and—"

"He was a dick."

"He manipulated her. She didn't willingly sleep with him."

"I know, I know. It's just..." She sighs and drops her head onto my shoulder. I want to feel happy about the fact that she's using me for comfort, but the truth is that she's just exhausted and overwhelmed. She's had so much to try to deal with and process in only a few days. It's no wonder she doesn't know what to deal with first.

"Just promise me you'll talk to her. Don't let him ruin your friendship."

"I promise."

The rest of the flight and the taxi drive into the

city are pretty quiet. We've both got too much on our minds to do much talking.

"It's on the right here," Lauren says, twisting in her seat, getting ready to get out.

I was less than impressed when she immediately gave the driver her and Joe's address when we got in, but I'm not sure what I was really expecting. This is her home.

The taxi pulls to a stop outside her building and my heart falls into my stomach. I'm not ready for our time together to come to an end already. I don't really feel like I've achieved all that much, other than the fact that all our words are no longer shouted at each other.

"Well...uh...thanks for gate crashing, I guess."

I think back to my journey through the airport to find her, and it feels like a lifetime ago, not three days.

"You're welcome. I hope I didn't totally ruin your time away."

"Not entirely. There were a couple of good bits."

"A couple?" I try to make it sound light and playful, but I seriously miss the mark.

Her sympathetic eyes turn on me and she smiles.
"Thank you, I think."

"Wait," I call just before the door closes. "When

can I see you again?" Her mouth opens to respond, but no words pass her lips. "I'm not giving up here, Lauren."

"I...I don't know. I'll call you in a couple of days, and we'll sort something out."

Before I get a chance to respond, the door's shut and she's walking away, tugging her small suitcase behind her.

"Fuck."

"Where to, mate?" the driver asks, ignoring my frustration. I rattle off Mum's address.

Resting my head back, my exhaustion takes over and I sleep the whole journey. The driver actually has to wake me up when he pulls up in front of the driveway.

"Shit, I'm sorry. How much do I owe you?"

I pay him and stagger out. I don't have anything; the few bits that Lauren picked up for me I either left behind or squeezed into her case.

Letting myself through the gates, I find both Mum and Chris' cars in the driveway. Thinking nothing of it, I unlock the front door and head towards the kitchen for a drink.

There's music playing somewhere in the house, but there are no voices, so the last thing I expect is to stumble upon two barely-dressed people locked in an embrace in the kitchen.

"Oh fuck. Shit. Sorry." Closing my eyes, I turn and walk away, trying to will the image of Chris' hands on my mum's body from my mind.

Flustered, panicked voices sound out from behind me before Mum's soft footsteps start getting closer.

"I'm so sorry. I didn't think you were back until tomorrow. I was—"

"Pre-occupied?"

She's clutching her silk robe tightly around her body in an attempt to cover up what she's wearing—or not—underneath. No grown man should have to see his mum in slutty lingerie; it's just wrong.

"Fuck," Mum whispers, looking up to the ceiling. "We...I...fuck—"

"It's okay, Mum."

"But—'

"But what?"

Back when Nick told me about her indiscretions when he was trying to get rid of me, I had no idea if she had cheated or whatever, but something told me that if it were true—and she's since pretty much confirmed that it was—it would be with Chris. They'd been friends for years, and although Mum fell in love with Dad, I always thought Chris was a little too attentive. "You're both consenting adults. I mean, I didn't need to witness...*that*. But what you do is up to you."

She lets out a giant breath. I don't understand why she was so worried, but then something Lauren said recently hits me. *I don't know who you are now.* Guilt sits heavy in my stomach that the reason Mum looks so relieved is my fault. It's true; they have no idea who I am now and how I'm going to react to things. Anger burns within me. I clench and unclench my working hand, trying to release some of the tension building.

"O-okay," Mum stutters, looking at me as if I might blow at any minute. "Did you have a good time with Lauren?"

"It was...good. Weird. But we talked. I think we've cleared the air at least."

"Good. That's good."

"I'm going to go." I point towards the stairs and turn to leave. "Keep the noise down, yeah?"

The sound of her light laughter behind me lifts my spirits a little. Chris sheepishly pokes his head from the kitchen just as I go to climb the stairs. One side of his mouth twitches up in a smile and I nod. "Just look after her." His smile grows as Mum tucks herself into his side, and I can't help my heart swelling a little. Has she moved on fast? Yeah, most people would probably say so, but then none of them knew the reality that was living with Nick. If Chris makes her smile, then who am I to criticise their choices? Fuck knows I've made enough bad ones over the years.

Undressing without Lauren to help me is a harsh reminder that she's across the city. At least I now know that she's not doing fuck knows what with her boyfriend. I still can't quite believe she lied to me, that she made me believe they were a couple, but looking back, I really should have seen the signs. I was too blindsided by her to see much else. Although, I could have sworn the look in his eyes every time he glanced at her went beyond friendship.

I'm just walking out of my en suite after attempting to shower while keeping my cast dry, when there's a light knock at my door.

"Come in."

"Hey," Mum says, poking her head inside. Thankfully, she's now fully dressed in her pyjamas. "Chris has just left."

"He didn't have to. I don't want to get in the way."

"No, it's fine. He was going anyway. Are you really okay with it?"

"Yes, I really am." She nods, but I don't think she believes me.

"Here," she says handing me a white paper bag. "I brought these home from the hospital for you. They might help with the pain." She nods to where I've got my arm wrapped around my ribs.

"Thanks." Ripping into the bag, I pop a couple of pills out of the packet and swallow them down, hoping they'll help me sleep tonight.

"Are you okay to talk, or do you need to rest?"

"We can talk." I slowly lower myself to my bed. Mum jumps up like she wants to help, but there's nothing she can really do. "What's up?"

Once I've found a somewhat comfortable position, I look over. She looks more concerned than she did after being walked in on earlier. "Word's got out at work that there are money issues."

"Shit." We were hoping to keep it quiet from the staff so they wouldn't panic unnecessarily. "What does that mean?"

"We've lost a few."

"Already?"

"The rumour's gone around that wages might not

be paid, and a few of the newer ones have jumped ship."

"Christ."

"Bert's also handed his notice in."

"Are you shitting me?" Bert worked with Steve on the contracts. We'll be fucked with both him and Steve gone.

"I tried to convince him to stay, but his son's set up on his own and he said it was the perfect time to support him."

"Fabulous. He's helping the competition," I say with a strained laugh. "What are we going to do?"

"Chris said he might know someone who could help?" I bite my tongue from asking what he knows about the building industry. I soon realise that I've no idea how to fix this, so if Chris knows a guy, then it's more than I've got. "Plus, I guess it frees up office space so we can—"

"Are the garages still full of Dad's crap?" I ask, remembering something Lauren said to me on the way home.

"Yeah, why?"

"What do you think about converting it into offices? We could apply for planning to extend to the side, so we'd have stores. It wouldn't be perfect, and it might not be a long-term solution, but it would save us some serious cash in the long run."

"I think..." She trails off, walking over to the window to look out at the driveway and the garages I mentioned. "I think we've got enough space for a few vans out there. We could pave some of the grass if need be. I think it's perfect, Ben."

"Are you sure? I don't want to crash your home, but it might be the new lease of life the business needs."

"It's not my home anymore, Ben. This place belongs to you, remember?"

"I know, but—"

"No buts. If you want to move the business here, that's your call to make. Just give me some warning before you decide to kick me out as well."

"I won't do that. This is your home."

"It was. It was my home when your dad was here with me. It's only been a house since then." The honesty in her voice makes my heart ache. I had no idea she felt the same way about this place that I did. "It deserves to be a home once again. I'd love nothing more than for you to raise a family of your own here."

A giant lump climbs up my throat at the idea of living here with Lauren and starting a life together. I've no idea what she sees for her future and if I'm in it, but I know exactly what I want, and it seems Mum does too.

I nod, unable to speak around the lump blocking my throat.

"I'll leave you to sleep. I just needed to tell you what was going on."

"I appreciate it. Thank you," I manage to get out before she leaves the room.

"Jesus," I mutter, rubbing my hand over my face.

The prescription painkillers Mum gave me work like a charm, because as soon as I find a semi-comfortable position, I'm out like a light.

CHAPTER TWELVE

Lauren

I DIDN'T ANTICIPATE how empty I would feel as I walk away from Ben. Everything inside me screams to turn around and go back to him, but I know I can't. That's my heart talking, and it's already got me in enough trouble where Ben Johnson is concerned. Before I let it have its way, my head needs to be certain that he's in it for real this time. I already know I won't survive the heartache if he walks away again and I've allowed myself to fall.

It's late Friday night and I expect the flat to be empty, so I'm shocked when I hear water running from Joe's room. He's usually out getting drunk and having the time of his life by now. I'm definitely the quiet one in our friendship while he's the wild child.

Propping my suitcase up in the hallway, I step into his room. "Hey, I'm back," I call but get no response. Glancing around, I take in the mess that I've become used to. Thankfully, he keeps it all confined to his room.

A stack of papers on his desk catches my eye. I shouldn't be spying, but the giant red FINAL DEMAND stamp on the top is kind of hard to miss. Walking over, my heart pounds when I see the logo for our letting agent at the top of the letter.

"What the fuck?"

Picking up the paper, I read words I never thought I would. Pay our outstanding rent arrears or face eviction. Joe hasn't been paying the rent?

"Oh, hey, you're back. Did you have...fuck." Racing over, he snatches the paper from my hand and screws it up. "Did you have a good time?"

"What the fuck was that, Joe?"

"It's nothing. You don't need to worry about it."

"I don't need to worry that we're about to be evicted? What the hell?"

"It's just a mistake. I'll sort it."

"Look me in the eye and tell me that," I demand when I notice that he's looking everywhere but me.

He turns his dark eyes on me, guilt etched into every one of his features, and I already know that this isn't a mistake. "I...fuck."

"I give you half of the rent every month. What the hell have you done with it?" Anger starts to bubble through my veins. I really fucking want this to be a joke, because I'm not sure I can deal with anything else right now.

"I spent it."

"All of it?"

"It was never an issue before, because the rent was covered."

"What do you mean the rent was covered? Who was paying for it?" I don't know why I ask. The tight knot in my stomach already knows.

"Lauren, this isn't how it sounds," he pleads, concern filling his eyes.

"You'll need to tell me before I figure that out."

"Fuck." Lifting his hands to his hair he runs his fingers through and tugs hard. "Fuck." I jump at the volume he shouts it at.

"Just tell me." My hands tremble as I wait for the inevitable to fall from his lips. "Who paid our rent?"

"Your dad," he mutters, and although I knew it

was coming, I still feel like the world just fell from under me.

I drop down onto the edge of Joe's bed as I try to figure out why.

"I didn't have any other option at the time, and your dad knew it." Frustrated with hearing the same words from so many people recently, I narrow my eyes and wait for him to continue. "My parents had disowned me. I had no money and nowhere to live. It was my only option if I didn't want to sleep on the streets."

My mind spins and blood rushes past my ears as what he's confessing registers. Sucking in a few deep breaths, I look up. Joe looks like hell when my eyes land on him, but it doesn't make me feel any better about all this.

"You're telling me what exactly? My dad paid you to be my friend?" My body trembles with anger as I wait for his response. Surely those words can't be true. Joe has been the kind of friend I could have only wished for, especially when we first became close. I'll be the first to admit that I wasn't in a great place back then...why would he want to spend time with me if he *weren't* being paid? A sob rumbles up my throat as I realise that it's true. He doesn't need to say the words; they're written all over his face.

"Lauren, it wasn't like that."

"Really? So what was it like?" Standing toe-to-toe with him, I wait. I wait for him to tell me that it's all a sick joke. But instead, he swallows and looks away. My eyes burn as the realisation that my relationship with my best friend is based on a lie really hits me. "I can't do this," I whisper, walking from his room and collecting my suitcase.

"Lauren, please. Let me explain. It's not as bad as it sounds," he begs.

"So my dad didn't pay you to be my friend?" I look back over my shoulder to find him in the doorway, guilt twisting his face. "Exactly."

"Lauren, please don't do this. I love you, please." His pained voice hits my ears as I wrench the front door open, but it doesn't stop me, and I storm through it. The lump in my throat is painful, and my eyes continue to burn, but I won't cry. Not until I'm in the safety of my car at least.

I didn't have a plan other than to get away, but when I find myself driving up the street where I know Ben is, I'm not surprised. The most sensible thing would be to go to Mum or Danni, but they're not who I want right now.

Before I change my mind, I pull up to the gates and slowly drive through once they're open. Looking up at the house and wiping the tears from my eyes, I realise I don't hate it like I once did. I don't really want to accept it, but since Dad passed, everything is just so…different. I'm not sure I can really explain it, but everyone is walking a little straighter, everyone's eyes are a little brighter. It's not that they're glad he's gone or anything…I don't think. It's more that the pressure he put on everyone has disappeared, and they're all feeling lighter. I can already see the difference in Jenny; she's becoming the woman I'm sure she always was; too busy hiding in Dad's shadows.

Turning off the engine, I start to question myself. I don't want to give him the wrong idea. He's desperate for us to re-start where we left off six years ago, but I need to protect my heart. That doesn't stop me needing his comfort after this latest revelation. The thought of having his strong arms wrapped around me right now is enough to have me pushing the car door open and heading towards the house.

Everything's quiet as I make my way up the stairs, but it's not an uncomfortable silence like I remember all too well.

Placing my hand on his door handle, I almost turn around and walk back out, but the image of Joe's guilt-ridden face has me pushing down instead.

The only light in the room is a small lamp on his bedside table. It allows me to clearly see him sleeping. I spot a box of painkillers beneath the lamp, and I realise that I shouldn't be here. Not just because I'm treading on dangerous ground with him, but also that he needs to sleep. He tried telling me that he slept fine in Rome, but I know he was lying. I heard him shuffling about and sucking in sharp, painful breaths as he tried to get comfortable. I need to walk out; but his peaceful, sleeping face has me lingering longer than I should. His bedroom is the same as I remember; the only difference is the man sleeping within it. I don't just mean physically. He always seemed so confident as a kid, but as we grew closer, I saw that most of that was a cover. He was hiding from the pain of losing his dad and acting out to make it seem like he'd dealt with it. He was lost back then. He didn't know his place in the world, and he just bumbled around, enjoying what he could. It's why I wasn't convinced that he really wanted me in the first place.

Ben the man seems much surer of himself. I know he's still got plenty of issues to deal with, my dad being one of them it seems, but to me at least, he's found where he needs to be. I know he's having a hard time leaving the life he's lived for the past six years and the friends he's made, but he knows as well as I do that he belongs here.

Letting out a sigh, I turn to leave.

"Lauren?" His voice is rough and gravelly, and it makes me stop in my tracks. I look back over my shoulder, and he stares at me like I can't possibly be standing here.

"I should go. This was a bad idea."

"No, wait." He gets up much more smoothly than I was expecting. The sight of the sheets slipping down his torso has me frozen in place. "Shit, what's wrong?"

Before I know it, he's in front of me, his thumbs wiping the tears from my cheeks.

"It's..." The security of his warmth seeping into me along with his scent filling my nose is too much. I lose the fight with my emotions, and a sob rumbles up my throat. "It's..."

I don't get a chance to say any more before I'm pulled against his hard body and his arms wrap around me. Dragging in a few deep breaths, I try to calm myself down. I'm fed up of falling apart and being such a mess, but it's just one thing after another right now. Every single thing is the result of one man's actions, and I'm really starting to dislike him.

I'm seeing a side to my dad that I should have seen when he was alive.

Some of this might not have happened if I didn't bury my head in the sand. I feel stupid and naïve for ever believing he was a man I could trust and who had my best interests at heart. All he wanted was to be in control. Another wave of tears hits, and Ben moves us over to his bed. His arms don't once leave me and the amount of comfort I find in that scares me.

"It's okay," he whispers, his lips in my hair. "I'm here for whatever you need."

"It's...Joe," I finally get out.

"What's happened? Is he okay?"

"Oh, he's fine. At the moment," I say, thinking that might not be the case when Ben catches up with him after this. Broken arm or not, I already know he's going to want to fight this battle for me.

Pulling his head back, he looks at me with his brows drawn. "What do you mean?"

"My dad paid Joe to be my friend. Everything between us has been based on a lie." My lips tremble as I say the words aloud.

Ben tenses beside me. "Motherfucker."

"I thought our relationship was just as important

to him as it was me, but he was only there because he was getting paid for the privilege."

Ben vibrates with anger. His eyes are dark, his lips pressed into a thin line and his jaw pops as he fights to stay here with me. "I'm gonna fucking kill him," he growls. Lust shoots through me at the sound of his deep voice. I may still have a lot of reservations about restarting a relationship with Ben, but one thing I do know for certain is that he will protect me, no matter what.

"No," I sigh, placing my hands on his chest. "I don't need you getting involved."

"What do you need?"

"I've no idea. Can I..." I trail off, not sure if I should be asking the question that's on the tip of my tongue.

"Can you what?"

"Can I stay?"

"This is your house too, Lauren. You don't need my permission."

"That isn't what I meant, and you know it. Can I stay?" I flick my eyes to his bed. "I don't want to be alone."

"You can have whatever you want, baby." His eyes darken, and I immediately regret asking. He wants more than I'm willing to give right now.

"Just hold me?" I look away, embarrassed by my request, but his fingers gently press into my chin and turn me back.

"Always."

Our eyes hold, and my mouth waters. It would be so fucking easy to lean into him right now. My fingers fist the sheet beneath me as I try to remind myself why I wanted to take this slow.

"I just need..." As I move, he releases his hold on me.

"Lauren," he calls just before I disappear into his bathroom. My breath catches when I look over my shoulder at him. His bruises are starting to fade and he looks incredible sitting there with the covers pooled at his waist. "Yeah?" I breathe.

"I mean it. Whatever you need. I'm here."

"I know." Ducking inside his bathroom, I close the door and take a breath. I was expecting to spend the evening at home alone as I dissected every second of our time together in Rome, but here I am, hiding in his bathroom. I couldn't even make two hours without him.

Shaking my head at my ridiculousness, I do what I need to do before splashing my face with cold water and attempting to brush my teeth with my finger.

Finding one of Ben's folded t-shirts on the side, I

run my finger over the cotton. Lifting it from its place, I bring it to my nose and inhale his scent. Butterflies erupt in my stomach and I can't stop myself.

Stripping out of my own clothes, I leave them in a pile on the floor and slip his shirt over my head. Something within me settles the moment I'm surrounded by him.

I run my fingers through my knotted hair and stare at my red-rimmed, tired eyes in the mirror. I'm fed up of all the bullshit and drama. I thought it was over, but it seems that was just wishful thinking.

The second I pull the door open, I'm less confident about my decision to borrow Ben's shirt, but I soon realise that I needn't worry because one look at him and I know he's out cold. A smile twitches at my lips that he's finally able to get some good rest as I make my way across the room. Pulling the covers back, I slip in beside him and run my eyes over every inch of his face. He's not shaved since the accident, so he's got five days' worth of growth covering his chin; if anything, it only makes him more beautiful. His dark eyelashes rest down on his strong cheekbones and his lips are curled into the slightest smile. The thought that I could have something to do with that causes heat to bloom inside me.

Leaning forward, I gently place my lips to his forehead. "Thank you," I whisper. I'm not sure what exactly it's for, but it feels right. He might have turned my world upside down once again when he reappeared, but I can't imagine dealing with the fallout of Dad's death without him.

There's no sign he's awake, but suddenly his arm moves, and he wraps it around my waist and pulls me to him. It feels so incredibly good to be wrapped in his arms once again.

CHAPTER THIRTEEN

Ben

I TRULY THOUGHT it was a drug-induced dream, so when I come to and hear the shower running in my en suite and the other side of the covers flicks back like I have company, I'm shocked.

The water stops and the sound of her light footsteps filters through the slightly ajar door. If I didn't know better, I'd think that was an invitation.

The moment her shadow fills the gap, my cock twitches to life. Propping myself up against the headboard, I wait. I'm not disappointed when she appears, because she's dressed in only my t-shirt.

"Fuck me. This is the best sight I've woken up to in a long time."

Her cheeks heat and she tugs at the hem. "Sorry, did I wake you?"

"No, not at all. I just wasn't expecting you to be here."

"You thought I'd run?" Confusion fills her voice.

"No. I thought it was a dream."

"I wish," she mutters sadly.

"Come here." To my surprise, when I open my arms for her, she comes willingly. Sitting on the edge of the bed beside me, she allows me to comfort her. Knowing she's accepting it—me, maybe even *us*—has some of the uncertainty within me settling. She came here to be with me last night. That means something. It means a lot, actually.

"Do you want to talk about it?"

She shakes her head, but after a few seconds, her soft voice fills the room. "I found a final demand letter for the rent. Dad was paying for it. I guess the payments stopped with all the financial issues. I had no idea. I was giving him my half every month. Christ knows what he's done with that. Unless we pay the outstanding debt, we're being evicted...next week." She shudders in my arms and I hold her a little tighter.

"I just can't quite get it into my head that after everything we've done together, how close I thought we were, he was only there for financial gain. It just doesn't make sense."

"You need to talk to him." She's silent in my arms, and it's clear she's got nothing to add. "It might make more sense if you found out more. I know for a fact that things aren't always that simple where your dad was concerned."

"I'm not ready. I can't cope with the fact that two of my best friends were manipulated by a man I used to love, who I thought, although controlling, was a good guy. I just don't know how to deal with it all. It's too much too soon."

"I know, baby. But I really think—"

"Take me away. Just for the weekend. Please. I need just a little time to try to process everything. Then I'll come back and talk to both Joe and Erica."

Placing my hand on her shoulder, I push her back so I can look in her eyes. I open my mouth to argue, but she beats me to it.

"Please, Ben. I've got my case from Rome in the car. We don't have to go far, just somewhere I know they're not going to find me. Please," she begs. Her blue eyes stare into mine, and I can see all the beautiful but broken pieces her dad's left behind.

"Okay," I concede. I've never been able to say no to her. "Let me get dressed and we'll make a plan."

"I'm not planning. Just take me somewhere. Anywhere." An idea pops into my head, and I smile.

"What?" she asks sceptically.

"I know just the place, and I can guarantee that you'll be distracted."

"Should I be worried?"

"Possibly," I admit with a laugh. "Now get dressed, unless you're planning on going in my t-shirt."

"WE'RE GOING AWAY for the night," I say to Mum, who's drinking coffee at the kitchen table and smiling down at her phone.

"But you just got back."

"I know, but—"

"It's my fault," Lauren says, walking around me and into the kitchen.

"Lauren? What are you doing here first thing in the morning?" Mum looks between the two of us with an amused expression plastered on her face.

"It's a long story. One that you'll probably not be surprised involves my dad."

"Now what?"

"Did you know that Dad and Joe knew each other prior to his employment?" I'd shown Lauren the other photos Liv sent me while we were away before leaving my room a few minutes ago. It only confirmed what she already knew.

"No, not that I know of. Why?"

"Dad paid him to be my friend. I guess to distract me from him," she says, nodding her head towards me.

"I'm sorry, he what?" Mum asks, spluttering coffee all over the table and down her chin.

"At some point, I might find someone in my life who hasn't been manipulated by my father."

Mum and I look at each other, and a knowing look passes between us at being two of those people.

"What's Joe got to say about all this?"

"I didn't hang around long enough to hear. It's just all too much. I just need a few hours to try to get my head straight. I thought dealing with his death would be hard, but all this other crap is just...ugh," Lauren complains. I can't help but feel for her. Losing a parent is one of the hardest things to deal with, even as an adult. I might not agree with her running away right now, but I do understand her need for time.

"Take whatever time you need, sweetheart. At a time like this, no one can tell you what you need. Only you know, so trust yourself and don't rush it. Grief is a bitch, and it can hit you when you least expect it. Things will get better though." Sadness fills Mum's eyes. She knows how true that is all too well.

"Thank you." I watch as Lauren walks over to give Mum a hug. It's the first time I really appreciate how close they became while I was gone.

They're only separated when the doorbell rings.

"Are you two expecting someone?" Mum asks, looking confused. We've never really had the kind of house that people just turn up to.

Shaking our heads, I leave them to find out who it is.

I'm pretty sure I already have a good idea. My muscles tense as I reach out to open the door. I might not be on top form right now, but I'm not opposed to kicking his arse.

"What?" I grunt the second my suspicions are confirmed.

"Can I see her?" Joe asks, looking tired and stressed.

Stepping out and closing the front door behind me, I focus my stare on him. "No, you fucking can't. What the fuck were you playing at? She fucking trusted you." My teeth grind as I fight the urge to punch the fucker. Sadly, I'd have to use my left hand, and I know it wouldn't hurt as much as I'd like it to.

"It's not like it seems," he pleads.

"Really. So Nick didn't pay you to be her friend? To distract her from me? I guess we can both see why he chose you. You're a weaker version of me. Wait... don't tell me. You're not gay either?" His eyebrows pinch together but he remains silent. "Yeah, I know."

"I don't...It's not..." With a sigh, he gives up. "She's my best friend; I love her. I couldn't give a fuck about her dad. Yeah, I needed him in the beginning. I was in a bad place, but it soon became clear that we had a connection."

"Then you should have fucking owned up. He's caused her enough pain trying to control her life over the years. You owed her the truth. It should have come from your own lips."

"Like you're one to give advice. At least he didn't run me out of London."

"Fuck you," I spit, lurching forward.

"Go on then. Fucking hit me."

"Enough," is called from behind us before Lauren's hands wrap around my upper arms to pull me back. "Ben, don't. He's not worth it." The pain that fills Joe's eyes at her words almost has me feeling bad for him. It's enough for me to know that what he just said is true. He does care about her. But it doesn't fix the fact he's lied to her for years.

"Joe, you need to leave."

"Lauren, please. Just hear me out."

"Not now."

"Please," he begs.

"Not. Now." Lauren spits, and Joe has no choice but to back away. "Are you okay?" she asks, turning her concerned eyes on me.

"Me? Yeah, I'm fine. Are you?" She shrugs before leading me back inside. "You really need to talk to him." I know she probably doesn't want to hear it, but I can't stop the words falling from my mouth. Why I'm defending the fucker is beyond me, but I truly believe he does care, and if he's done as good a job as I think he has of looking after her for the last few years then he deserves to be heard.

Mum's stood in the hallway waiting to see what's going on, concern written all over her face. "Just do what feels right," she says to Lauren with a small smile before heading up the stairs.

"Let's go." Turning, she locks her eyes on mine.

"You sure?"

"Yes. Now take me away, Ben."

"Fine, you're driving."

"Just point me in the right direction."

"WE'RE GOING TO DEVON, aren't we?" she asks the second we're on the motorway heading out of the city.

"Is that okay?"

"Stop questioning everything," she says with a chuckle. "I told you I didn't care where we went, and I meant it."

"I just want to make you happy."

"This is making me happy." She might not say that I'm the one making her happy in so many words, but hope explodes within me nonetheless. "I'm looking forward to meeting your friends properly."

The journey is fairly quiet, and I allow Lauren the time she needs to process everything that's whizzing around her head. It's late afternoon when I direct her to pull up on the driveway of Dec's house.

"Whoa, when you said you looked out on the beach, I wasn't quite expecting this. It's incredible."

"Dec was really lucky to get this place."

"I can't believe you wanted to leave in favour of London."

"It wasn't the place that was calling me back."

She turns the engine off and shifts in her seat so she can look at me. "My home is wherever you are." Her breath catches and her eyes soften. I expect her to say something, but after a few seconds, she just smiles. "Are you ready? This lot can be a little crazy."

"Worse than those we left behind?"

"No, probably not," I admit with a laugh, thinking of Erica and a few of the others.

"Holy shit, Ben!" Liv cries the second I step foot into the living room. She jumps up and runs towards me. She's just about to collide with me when she takes in the cast. By some miracle, she manages to stop before she hits me and gently wraps her arms around my waist. "What's happened? Are you okay? What's going on with Lauren?" She fires the questions out without giving me a chance to answer any of them.

"Nothing, she's right here," Lauren says from behind me, causing Liv's eyes to go so wide I'm worried they might pop out.

"Oh my god!" Liv turns her attention to Lauren and gives her the overenthusiastic hug I was almost about to get. "Can I get you drinks?"

"Sure."

We follow Liv through to the kitchen. I can see Lauren looking around at everything out of the corner of my eye. It feels weird being back here, and even weirder having her with me. I never thought I'd ever have my two worlds become one, but it seems that it might just be happening.

Liv puts the kettle and coffee machine on and then turns her attention to us. "So are you two..."

"Friends," Lauren answers quickly.

"Friends?" Liv's eyes flick between the two of us before landing on me. "How's that working for you?"

"Fantastic, I love being Lauren's friend," I say through gritted teeth, which earns me a slap to the shoulder.

"Behave," Lauren chastises. "He's trying."

"You have some weird power over our BJ, that's for sure." Lauren stifles a laugh while Liv just looks amused. "I never thought I'd see him whipped."

"Enough. Don't make me regret bringing her here."

"No, please continue. I really want to learn more about the elusive BJ," Lauren encourages, and I groan.

"You really don't."

"Okay, no, I don't want to know about *that* side to BJ."

Liv and Lauren chat away like they're old friends. Neither seems to be even slightly concerned that I'm in the same room as they talk about me and compare notes.

"Babe, whose car is parked in the...BJ!" Liam exclaims as he rounds the corner. "Dude, it's good to see you. Lauren, hey, this is a surprise. Are you two...?"

Liv pierces him with a look while running her hand in front of her throat to get him to stop, and it works...eventually. "They're just friends. I'm going to make up the guest room for her."

"Wow, BJ has a woman here, and she's not going to share his bed. What a novelty."

"Shut up, dickhead."

"Ow," Liam complains, rubbing the sting my hand left behind on his head. "I had years of stick off you; it's time for payback."

"I was afraid of that," I mutter.

"So what's the plan? The shack to meet Dec and Nic?"

"Yes. Let me show Lauren to her room so she can get ready."

The girls disappear up the stairs. Liam and I watch them leave before I head up to my old room to shower and dress. The painkillers Mum got from the hospital mean I can move a little easier, and getting dressed isn't quite as agonising as it was in Rome.

I'm hit with a huge wave of nostalgia when I open my bedroom door and find it exactly as I left it the day I headed for London. I think back to the uncertainty I felt that day. I had no clue what I was about to walk into. In reality, I think it's worse than I was expecting—business-wise at least. But Lauren's single and mostly open to us again, even if she is trying to fight it.

As soon as I'm ready, I head back downstairs and find Liam at the table nursing a beer where I left him. The second he sees me heading his way, he grabs me a can so I can join him.

"So...friends? How's that working out for you?"

I groan in pain and a smug smile spreads across Liam's face. "Oh, just fuck off."

He laughs but his face soon turns serious. "She just needs time. You two are it, and you know it."

"Yeah." A sad laugh falls from my lips. "I know it. I'm just not sure she does."

"She does. I can see it in her eyes every time she looks at you." I narrow my eyes at my best friend, wondering when he turned into a love doctor. "What?"

"Nothing, nothing. So, how're things down here?"

"Quiet. This house just isn't the same without

you. What are your plans now? Have you moved to London officially?"

I look around the house that I called home for years and realise that I can no longer call it that. "Yeah, I guess I have."

"This place was too small for you anyway."

"I guess," I say sadly. As much as starting over with the business and Lauren in London excites me, I'm also sad to say goodbye to this place. It might never have been where I was meant to be, and I never fitted in, not really, but I've got some amazing memories of my time here—not to mention some incredible friends.

"Distance doesn't mean shit when...fuck." Liam's distracted when footsteps hit the bottom step and he looks over to Liv. She looks good in a little playsuit thing, her legs going on for miles. I understand why he lost his train of thought.

He gets up and goes straight over to her, ruining her perfectly applied lipstick.

"Where's Lauren?"

"Coming," Liv mumbles against Liam's lips.

Exactly as she said, footsteps descend the stairs and I wait. A pair of sandals appears before a tanned pair of legs has my mouth watering. Slowly, the rest of her is revealed. She's wearing a sexy little floral dress that hugs her body in the most delicious way. I swallow and shift on my seat as I will my cock not to go full mast just from looking at her. Once she's down, I take in her loosely curled hair and simple make-up. She looks fucking stunning, and I realise that tonight's going to be torture. Her eyes find mine, and something crackles between us. I may be the other side of the room, but I can sense the hitch in her breathing as our connection holds.

"Okaaaay," Liv says, trying to break the tension. "Ready to go?"

Liam gestures for Lauren to head out and I expect him to grab onto Liv, but she manages to give him the slip so she can grab me. "You're welcome," she says with a wink, nodding towards Lauren.

"This is painful."

"Yeah, I noticed that cast was on your writing hand. I bet you're having a hell of a time right now." She tries to contain her amusement but fails miserably. "Sorry, I'm sorry. You're totally winning her over, just so you know. She might put you out of your misery soon." As she says that, Lauren looks over. Our eyes lock again and a bolt of lust hits me so strong it makes my knees buckle.

Jesus Christ, I need her.

CHAPTER FOURTEEN

Lauren

BEN'S EYES have been glued to me since the moment I stepped down the stairs. His stare had goosebumps covering my skin and tingles shooting around my body. Every time I'm away from him, I tell myself that the next time I see him will be different, that the crazy connection between us is just in my head. But then I step into the same room as him and all my good intentions go to shit, because just like when I was eighteen, he has this power over me.

Liam walks beside me as we head towards the beach, leaving Ben and Liv trailing behind. Their hushed voices just about carry to us, and I can only imagine that Ben's getting quizzed about me. Seeing Ben with his friends settles something inside me. Although I hated him when he left, and I still do a little now, it makes me happy to know that he had people looking out for him when he was without family. My thoughts turn back to Joe, and my shoulders sag. I'm having a hard time believing that our friendship is based on nothing but lies and deceit, but that seems to be the level my dad functioned on so I'm not sure why I'm surprised.

"So, what was he like as a kid?" Liam asks, dragging me from my thoughts.

"I uh...didn't know him as a kid. Our parents married when I was fifteen, and we never really spent any time together until I moved in at eighteen."

"I hear you spent quite a bit of time together then," he says, giving my arm a nudge.

"Yeah," I sigh.

"Shit, I'm sorry. I didn't mean—"

"It's fine, it's fine." It's really not, but I don't want to bring a downer on what should be a fun night. "He hasn't changed all that much since back then. He's just a little more focused, I guess. He was always a bit of a joker, but he's more determined now. It's like he knows what he wants and he'll do whatever it takes to make it happen."

"You're talking about yourself, right?" My cheeks heat under his stare. "You know he won't stop." I can see that Liam wants to say more, probably to ask me how long I'm going to string his mate along for, but thankfully, he keeps his mouth shut. "Here we are."

"This place is incredible." I look around, taking in the perfect sandy beach with the sun setting in the distance, casting everything in an orange glow.

"Lauren?" Ben's deep voice rolls through me. I turn to look at him, and concern covers his face—that is until I smile at him and it lights up. I'm reminded of everything he's done for me in the last few days, and it chips away a little more of my restraint.

Stepping into his side, he wraps his arm around my shoulder and drops a kiss to my head. Heat fills me and I snuggle in deeper.

"Is this okay?"

"It's perfect."

Together we walk into Dec's beach shack. It looks exactly as I would have imagined, if not better.

Dec and Nic get up from the sofa to greet us.

Dec pulls Ben into a very gentle man hug while Nic comes over to me.

"It's so good to see you again."

Her wide smile makes guilt twist my stomach as I think back to the last time I saw them. It wasn't exactly an enjoyable experience as Ben and I squared up to each other in the club.

"I promise to cause less drama this time."

"We live in a sleepy little town; we love a bit of drama here."

I'm ushered over to the bar with Liv and Nic while the guys make themselves comfortable on the sofas, looking out at the beach beyond.

The three of us watch them catching up and laughing together.

"How's he really doing?" Liv asks.

"What, aside from the fact that he fell from the roof of a building?"

"Yeah, we can see how he's doing with that," she says with a laugh.

"He's okay, I think." I hate that I can't really answer with confidence. I've been so lost in my own head that I don't really know where his head is at. "He's got a lot of work on his hands with the business. My dad did a really good job screwing everything up."

"If anyone can do it, BJ can."

Pride swells within me at their words. "Yeah, he can." Looking over at him laughing and joking with his friends, friends who have been his family for the past six years, makes my heart ache. There's so much of his life and who he is that's a mystery to me, and I hate it. I want to know him like I did back in the beginning, not have this huge void between us.

He must be able to feel my stare because he looks over. Something crackles between us and my temperature rises.

Nic waits until he's turned away and joined back in with the guys' conversation before she speaks. "We've never seen BJ like he is with you. It's something we really never thought we'd see." I look between the two of them, urging them to continue. I'm desperate to know more about the Ben they know. "He was..." Nic pauses as she thinks. "A little...free and easy—"

"Manwhore," Liv chips in helpfully. "What?" she asks when Nic gives her a hard stare. "Lauren knows the basics, and I don't think she wants us sugar coating. Right?" she asks, turning to me.

"Right," I agree, even if the idea of discussing Ben with other women makes me want to throw up.

"I really didn't ever think I'd see him hung up on

one woman. I think it looks good on him." I don't need to turn around to know that he's looking at me once again. My skin burns with his attention. "He really loves you, Lauren."

A giant lump forms in my throat. I nod because that's all I'm capable of before swiping my wine from the counter and swallowing a huge mouthful. I know how Ben feels. I can see it every time I look into his eyes. I just wish I wasn't so afraid to have my heart broken again.

"I know you both probably think I'm stringing him along but—" I let out a sigh as I try to find the right words.

"You don't have to explain anything to us. We know all too well how complicated these things can be," Liv says, placing a comforting hand on my arm.

I smile sadly at her. "He shattered my heart when he left. I know I won't survive if it happens again."

"None of us can predict the future, Lauren, but we can regret the past. Don't waste time if you think it's something you'll look back on later and regret."

Her words hit with the punch I think she intended.

"Are they playing nice?" Ben asks when the girls

get distracted by their boyfriends and I find myself accompanied by him at the bar.

"Yeah, they're lovely. They were dishing the dirt on you. I've been learning what a dog you were." He swallows nervously. "I'm kidding, but I'm assuming from your reaction that it's not far from the truth."

"The less we discuss my antics here the better." The image of him touching faceless women once again pops into my head. "You want to get out of here?"

"Only if you're ready."

"I am. I don't want to share you anymore."

"Is that right?" Butterflies erupt in my stomach at the prospect of it just being the two of us. I try my best to put the little bit of lingering doubt I have aside.

After saying our goodbyes, Ben links his fingers with mine and we head out into the night.

"Isn't the house that way?" I ask when he tugs me in the opposite direction and then down onto the sand.

"I thought we could just walk for a bit."

"Okay, hang on." Coming to a stop, I lean against the wall and slip my shoes from my feet. The cool sand seeps between my toes as I gather my sandals and reach for Ben's hand.

It's the perfect night. The sky's filled with twinkling stars and the sea gently crashes against the sand.

"Are you warm enough?" Ben asks, pulling me into his side and wrapping his good arm around me.

"Uh huh," I mumble, too content right now to ruin it with words. It was a lovely late summer's day, and although it's getting cold fast, with him beside me I'm fine.

We seem to walk for the longest time in silence, enjoying each other's company. It feels so good to just be after all the arguments and bullshit.

"It's really beautiful here," I eventually say, breaking the quiet night. "Are you sure you're ready to leave?"

"I'm going to miss it, that's for sure. The beach, the peace and quiet, the sea air."

"You know you don't have to, right? Just because everything's been left to you, it doesn't mean you have to deal with it. If this is your home then…" I trail off, not really wanting to voice the rest of that sentence.

Ben slows to a stop and pulls me in front of him. Tucking a lock of hair behind my ear, he stares into my eyes. It's like he can see right inside me and read all my fears.

"My home is wherever you are, baby."

My heart pounds at his honesty. It might not be the first time he's said it, but I'm starting to really believe him now. It might be foolish, but Liv's words are still on repeat in my mind.

I try not to think about what I'm doing and reach up on my tiptoes and press my lips to his. He sucks in a breath of surprise but soon accepts my kiss. His arms wrap around my waist and I'm pulled tightly against him as his lips part and his tongue dances with mine.

We kiss like it's the first time in six years. It's exactly how our first one should have been, instead of the angry, punishing one we shared at the time. Suddenly his words about home being wherever I am make sense, because right now, wrapped in his arms, with his lips on mine, this is home. A contented moan rumbles up my throat as I cling onto him tighter and kiss him deeper.

When we eventually break apart, our chests are heaving and his eyes are glassy with lust.

"W-we should get back," Ben whispers, his forehead pressed against mine, our bodies still woven together.

I hate the moment he releases me. It leaves me cold and I immediately want to step back into him.

The walk back is just as silent as before, and my concerns and doubts about what he's thinking and feeling start running rampant.

"I can practically hear you worrying."

"I am not," I argue.

"Really?" he says with a laugh.

We come to a stop at my bedroom door for the night, and I see Ben look over to his own longingly.

"Thank you for bringing me here, for showing me this side to you."

"You're welcome. You still like me with this side?" The little hesitation in his voice has me stepping closer.

"I like all of you, Ben. You don't need to worry about that. We all have things we wish we'd done differently; but looking back doesn't achieve anything."

"I know. I'll never forgive myself for walking away from you."

Placing my palm on his rough cheek, I look up into his dark-blue eyes. "At some point you're going to have to accept it, Ben. What happened... happened. You came back, and we can still write our future."

"Yeah?" Hope blooms in his eyes and my desire gets the better of me. My lips find his and I pull him against me. His cock almost immediately hardens against my stomach as the intensity of his kiss deepens.

"Jesus," he moans when I start kissing across his jaw and down his neck. My hand slips around from his back and I rub him over the fabric of his jeans.

The moan that rips from his lips has the ache between my legs almost unbearable.

Warm fingers wrap around my wrist and stop my movements. Ben dips his head and I shiver as his breath tickles my ear. "Don't start something you can't finish, baby."

"I can—" His fingers press against my lips, stopping any more words.

"The next time we're together, it's because I've proved to you that I mean every word I say. I want it to be the start of us, of our future. I want it to be because you're in this for real and not because you feel like you have to."

"I don't—" His lips cut me off and I start to believe he's changed his mind.

"Goodnight, baby." He releases me and walks down the corridor. I might think he's happy about this if it's not for the pained look on his face when he stops and glances back at me.

"Ben, I—"

"Sleep tight."

A long breath leaves me when his door clicks shut, cutting us off from each other. I follow suit and close mine too before leaning back against it and wondering how the hell I'm meant to fall asleep after that.

CHAPTER FIFTEEN

Ben

THE TENSION in Lauren's body increases the closer we get to London. I know she doesn't want to go home and deal with everything, but I'm not letting her run away any longer. As much as I'd love to keep her all to myself, we've both got things that need to be done. I've got a business that really needs my attention, and she's got two friends to speak to and decisions to make about her future. I haven't said any more about her coming back to work since we were on the plane. As much as I'd love for her to come back and work beside me, I'm not about to force her.

She had enough of that from her dad over the years. If she feels that now's the time for a fresh start, then so be it.

"This is you then," she says, pulling up in front of the house. Her voice is full of sadness and I'd do almost anything to help get rid of it, but she really needs to go home and get everything out in the open.

"Thank you for everything. Can I call you later?"

"Do you really need to ask that?"

"I guess not."

"If you need me, I'll be here, but no running away. You'll feel better once you've talked through everything."

Leaning over, I give her a quick kiss. It's nothing like what my body's craving, but it's all I can get away with right now. The memory of how her curves felt pressed up against my body last night is still at the forefront of my mind. I've no doubt that if I hadn't stopped her, I'd have ended up in her bed, but I knew it wasn't the right thing to do. I'd agreed to give her time to figure shit out, and I was determined to do the right thing...this time, at least.

"I'll see you soon." I try to sound positive as I get out of the car and grab my bag from the boot. I watch as she lets out a huge sigh before backing off the drive. She asked me to go with her, but I stand by my decision that she needs to do this alone. Me being there will only get Joe's back up.

"Hey, I'm home," I call once I'm in the house, hoping that it will stop a repeat of the last time I turned up unannounced.

"In the kitchen."

"Fully dressed?"

"It's safe," Mum shouts with a laugh. When I round the corner, I find Mum and Chris aren't alone—there's another man sitting with them, drinking coffee. "Hey, sweetheart, did you have a good time? Where's Lauren?" she asks peering around my shoulder, expecting her to appear.

"Gone home to deal with Joe."

"Oh...okay. Well, this is Trey, the man Chris suggested might be a good fit for us." It takes me a few seconds to catch up with what she's talking about. My drug-hazed brain had mostly forgotten the conversation I'd had with her when we got back from Rome about employees handing their notice in and finding someone new for the office.

"Hi. Your mum was just telling me all about you." Trey says, holding his hand out towards me. He's older than me, probably mid to late thirties, but he's a similar build, and I can see that we share a love of ink from the black intricate patterns poking out from his sleeves. His face is hard, his lips set in a slight scowl, and I can't help thinking he must be an arsehole of a boss. I'm not sure I'd want to be on the wrong side of his temper.

"All good I hope."

"Of course." I join them at the table while Mum faffs around getting more drinks. "So, I was just telling your mum a little about me..." he continues on to tell me his employment history within the building industry. I can't help find it odd that this man, who clearly looks capable, and I have every confidence that he is if Chris is vouching for him, is selling himself to me; the guy who's not held down a proper job since he walked out of this house over six years ago but suddenly finds himself in charge of a failing company. Everything sounds perfect; his experience is second to none, and I think he's got the attitude and determination it'll take to help me drag this company back from the dead.

"Sounds perfect. When can you start?" I ask with a laugh, but in reality I couldn't be any more serious. The prospect of being the boss is more daunting than I'm allowing anyone to see, but with the knowledge I have someone who knows what they're doing by my side with regards to running jobs and dealing with employees, the challenge suddenly seems a little more manageable.

Trey looks a little sceptical but eventually says, "Tomorrow?"

I'm too stunned to respond but Mum does it for me. "Done. Now, shall we have something a little more appropriate to celebrate? I feel like this could be the start of a new chapter for all of us."

When I fall into bed later that night, it's with hope filling my veins. Lauren seems to be softening to the idea of an 'us' again, and we've got some solid plans for how to save the business. I believe what Mum said earlier is true. This really is a turning point, and we're all about to find out if we're going to sink or swim.

CHAPTER SIXTEEN

Lauren

MY HAND TREMBLES as I lift it to slide the key in the lock. I really don't want to be forced to deal with all this bullshit and manipulation, but I know Ben's right. I need to get everything out in the open with both Erica and Joe and see where we go once all the truths are on the table. I'm terrified that my relationships with two of my closest friends are going to be forever tarnished by my dad's selfish actions, but I guess it's something we're all going to have to live with now.

Pushing the door open, I'm met by two shocked

faces as they put photo frames and ornaments into boxes. "If I didn't know better, I'd think this was an ambush."

"We didn't know…shit," Joe says, looking down at the boxes at his feet.

"Moving out?"

"Erica offered me her spare room until I sort myself out. I didn't know when you'd be back, so we just started. You didn't answer any of our calls and—"

"It's fine, really. You need to do what you need to do. I guess I'll go pack too."

"Where will you go?"

I shrug. "Do you care?"

"Jesus, Lauren." His hands go to his head and he pulls at his hair. "Of course I care. You're my best friend."

"Am I? Because the last I heard, your position was a fully paid job."

"It's not like that. Please, just come and sit down and let me explain."

Knowing it's the reason I'm here, I do as he suggests.

"Shall I go or…" Erica says, standing awkwardly in the corner of the room.

"No, if we're going to do this, we should do it properly. Sit."

"I'll get the wine," Joe suggests, disappearing into the kitchen.

"Did you know?" I snap at Erica when she sits on the sofa opposite me.

"No, I had no clue until he turned up at my door on Friday night. I'm so sorry, Lauren. But he's a mess. He really loves you."

"This is so fucked up."

"You're telling me. But just hear him out. Hear *me* out. There's too much good here to allow *him* to ruin everything."

I agree, I do, but the last thing I want to do is spend my Sunday night hearing tales about what an arsehole my dead Dad was.

Joe comes back, and if it's possible, the atmosphere gets even heavier. We all take a sip of wine, putting off the inevitable, but it can only last so long.

"Nick was a friend of my parents. I've known him for as long as I can remember. But as the years went on they drifted apart as people do. Everything you know about the beginning of how we met is true. I really did turn up that day after seeing an ad online for a job. I was desperate. My parents had kicked me out and cut me off after I 'shamed' them. I was never expecting to find Nick sitting in the office. I hadn't seen or heard from him for years. He sat me down and interviewed me like he would any other employee before he started asking about my parents. I gave him a shortened version about what had happened and he offered to help. I thought he was just being friendly, but it turned out to be far from that. He told me he'd push me up through the ranks, pay me more and even put a roof over my head if I did one thing for him."

"Be my friend," I mutter.

"It wasn't even that." He lets out a sigh and casts his eyes to the ceiling. "He wanted me to distract you in any way I could."

"Distract me?"

"He was concerned that you were going to go running after Ben. I think he took one look at me, another bad boy with tattoos, and thought I could make you forget him. Nick knew my parents. He knew that although I was going through a rough patch, I had 'good blood' or whatever bullshit he spewed."

"I can't believe you agreed," I say, shaking my head at how ridiculous it all sounds.

"Why wouldn't I? I had no money and nowhere to live. I'd been sleeping on friends' sofas but the offers were drying up fast once they realised I could no longer fund the booze and drugs. Plus, Lauren's hot...why wouldn't I want to spend my time with her?" he adds with a laugh.

"You should have told me, Joe."

"I wanted to. I intended to. But I soon realised that I really liked you, despite you being a miserable bitch and pining after Ben."

"Thanks."

"Would you put it any differently?"

"No."

"You quickly became my best friend, Lauren. You truly did, and I didn't know how to tell you then. You'd already had your trust smashed, and I just couldn't do it to you."

"So you just kept up the façade?"

"Yeah. I kind of thought your dad would get fed up with paying for this place once he realised you'd moved on with your life, but he never did. So I continued spending my wages every month—and your rent," he adds with a wince, "and here we are."

"Didn't you think to do something when you started getting late payment notices?"

"I mentioned it to Nick and he said he'd sort it. I had no idea he had no money."

"Jesus, this is such a mess."

"I'm so sorry, Lauren. I never had any intention

of hurting you. I was just in the right place at the right time. Maybe it was wrong of me to agree, but I don't regret it because it brought me you. I might have been there to support you as a distraction for you, but you were the same thing to me, and I'll forever be grateful for our friendship, even if you don't forgive me."

"Forgive you? Don't be stupid." Getting up, I sit myself down next to him. "You should have told me sooner. If I'd known what he was capable of, a lot of other things might have gone differently." I glance over at Erica and she gives me a sad smile.

The three of us talk for hours. Thankfully the topic of conversation steers away from my dad and it almost feels like old times. Sadly, one look at the boxes surrounding us and I'm brought back down to earth with a bang.

"So what now?" I ask.

"Now, we start over without the lies and secrets."

"That sounds like a plan, but you're moving in with Erica and I'm about to lose my home."

"We sort of assumed that you and Ben..." Erica trails off.

"We're not together."

"Why not? Lauren, he looks at you like you're the most amazing thing to ever grace the earth. He loves you so much; it's obvious every time he glances your way. It's been that way since you were eighteen. Put the poor boy out of his misery!"

Both Erica and Joe stare at me, waiting for my response. I open my mouth to say something, to argue, but nothing comes out.

"You know we're right," Joe adds, but I don't miss the sadness that darkens his eyes. "That man would move heaven and earth for you."

I can't fight the smile that twitches at the corners of my mouth. I can't argue with Joe, and I'm starting to realise that I need to be brave. I can hide all I like, but at the end of the day, I'll regret not having this time with him. Even if it all comes crashing down again, knowing my fears kept me from living life to the full with Ben would haunt me forever.

"Do you want some help packing?"

A few hours later, our flat is totally packed. It didn't take long to realise that we didn't have all that much stuff to begin with.

"I'm so sorry it came to this," Joe says, regret written all over his face.

"It is what it is. I think we could all use the fresh start, don't you?" Both Joe and Erica nod sadly as we each collect the last few things to carry down to our cars. The only thing left is furniture, which Joe says he'll collect tomorrow in a work van—as long as the boss agrees.

I tell myself I'm not going to cry as the three of us stand in the car park. Nothing's changing, not really. We're all still friends. Yes, our relationships might be a little more strained than they once were, but things will get better again with time.

"This is stupid," I say, my voice heavy with emotion as tears sting the backs of my eyes. "I'll see you both soon."

Two sets of arms wrap around me, and I lose the fight with my tears.

"I'm so sorry," they say simultaneously, and a sob bubbles up my throat.

In the space of only a couple of weeks, my life has completely changed. I lost a man I thought was a caring father, only to discover he was controlling my life every step of the way. The love of my life, who smashed my heart to smithereens, reappeared and turned my life upside down again, and I almost lost two of my best friends in the process. Things can only get better, right?

When I drive away from our building, it's with a heavy heart, but I can't deny there's a little bit of excitement for what's to come. Everyone I love gets a shot at a new start. I just hope they make the right choices this time around.

The logical part of my brain is screaming that I should be heading in the opposite direction—going to stay with Mum until I sort myself out would be the simplest and safest option—but I find myself heading towards a house I never thought I'd willingly want to live in again.

I hated that house when I was first forced to move in. I still hated it the day I moved out to live with Joe. Although it held some good memories of my time with Ben, seeing him everywhere I looked was so painful. Dad was totally out of order with what he did with Joe, but it was like he knew exactly what I needed. I guess in a way I was lucky that the guy he paid to be my friend was a decent guy who, despite the reason he was there, had a good heart.

Pulling up onto the driveway, images of the time I spent here with Ben run through my mind, from that very first night when he was an arsehole to me in the kitchen all the way to how he supported me on Friday night when I found out about Joe. A smile twitches my lips and I know I made the right decision coming here. It's time to start this new chapter in our lives, and I need to stop being so afraid and enjoy what's right in front of me.

Pushing the front door open, the sounds from the TV filter through to me. I slip my shoes off, drop my bag to the side and head into the house to find everyone.

As I round the corner into the living room, I find Jenny and Chris cuddled up on one sofa; the sight of them makes my breath catch. Ben had told me about their relationship when we were in Devon, and although I'm okay with Jenny moving on, I can't deny it doesn't sting a little that it's not my dad she's sat with.

"Oh, hey, sweetheart. Is everything okay?"

Her voice drags Ben's gaze away from whatever they're watching. His eyes burn into me the second they land on my body, and his brow creases with concern. He goes to get up but pauses when I speak.

"Yeah, yeah I'm fine. I was just wondering if I could ask you a favour?"

"Of course."

"Could I...uh...move back in?"

The skin around Jenny's eyes crinkles in delight as a wide smile spreads across her face. "I'm not sure, sweetheart." My stomach drops, and I suddenly feel stupid for even asking. This isn't my home anymore. Dad's gone, and I'm no longer part of this family. Tears sting my eyes and I'm about to turn when she speaks again. "This house no longer belongs to me. It should be Ben you're asking."

Turning my attention to him, I don't get a chance to say anything because his wide chest is in front of me. His arms wrap around my waist and I'm lifted off my feet. His lips find mine as he backs us out of the room.

"Turn the TV up," he shouts over his shoulder, and although my face flames red, I throw my head back and laugh. It feels so incredibly good to just let go and allow my heart to take the lead for the first time in six long years.

"I can walk," I offer. Ben must be regretting his decision to try to carry me up the stairs with one arm.

"I'm not letting you go." His words make me melt. I drop my face into the curve of his neck and start peppering kisses along the hem of his t-shirt. "That's not making it any easier," he chuckles.

By the time we get to his room, sweat is beginning to bead his brow, showing that carrying me up here isn't as easy and pain-free as he's making out.

"Put me down," I demand. The conviction in my tone is enough that he does as I say and slides me down his body. Taking his still unshaven cheeks in my hands, I stare up into his eyes. "You're in pain.

We've got all the time in the world. You don't need to rush this."

"You've no idea how long I've waited for this."

"Don't I? I ask, quirking a brow up.

"Come on." Threading his fingers through mine, he starts tugging me forward. "You're aware that you moving in comes with one condition?"

"What's that?"

"You're moving into my room."

Pushing his door open, he hurries inside. The second the door slams shut, I'm pressed up against it.

His palm glides up my neck and to my cheek, his fingers tangling into my hair. "Is this it?" His eyes bore down into mine, their intensity has my insides quivering.

I nod once but it's all the confirmation he needs. "I won't let you regret it...me." Then his lips are on mine and his body is pressing mine into the door. A whimper rumbles up my throat as his tongue slides against mine, tasting me, reminding him how good we are together.

My body sags against his, but he senses it. His knee presses between my legs, and along with his hips, he keeps me upright as his kiss continues.

Pulling his lips from mine, he kisses across my jaw and down my neck. My chest heaves with my increased breaths and I hungrily suck in some deep lungfuls of air.

"I never thought I'd get this again. Jesus, Lauren. Fuck." His hand brushes down my body and slips inside my jumper. "I need more. I need everything."

His fingers skim across my stomach before he finds the button holding my jeans closed. He makes quick work of popping it open, and in seconds, he's sliding his fingers inside and past the lace covering what he wants.

"Fuck," he grunts when he finds me wet and ready for him.

His fingers circle my clit, and quiet whimpers and begs for more fall from my lips. "Ben, please," I moan as he circles my entrance, teasing me.

My orgasm is just in reaching distance when he stills and pulls his hand from my jeans.

"I need to be inside you right now." He undoes his own trousers and pushes them and his boxers down his thighs. His cock bobs in front of him, the head purple and already glistening at the tip. "Lauren," he growls, and I manage to come back to myself enough to shimmy out of my jeans and knickers.

"I don't think you should be—"

My words are cut off as he wraps his hand

around my thigh and hitches it up to give him the space he needs. With his hand wrapped around his cock, he bends his knees and lines us up.

We both moan as he sinks into me. My walls ripple around him and the pleasure takes over my entire body. I've no idea if his moan was in pleasure or pain, or a little of both.

Dragging my eyelids open, I look up at him. All his muscles are pulled tight, his eyes locked on me as he starts to thrust in and out of me. I want to ask if he's okay, but he hits me deeper and I lose all train of thought. The only thing I can focus on is him and the sensations he's causing within me.

"So fucking good," he grunts, his movements never faltering. "I want to feel you, baby. Show me how good it feels having me inside you." His words, along with his thrusts, push me higher and higher, closer to my release.

Wrapping my arms tighter around his shoulders, I try to take a little more of my weight to help him. It changes our angle slightly and my orgasm hits, taking me by surprise. I cry out his name as he picks up the tempo a little. Dropping his head into the crook of my neck, I feel him swell inside me before he growls and releases everything he has.

We stay exactly as we are for the longest time, locked in our embrace and him softening inside me.

"Are you okay?" I whisper eventually.

Pulling his head up, he looks down at me. He's eyes are alight, and any tension that was on his face previously has gone. "I can honestly say I've never been better." The smile that splits his face melts my heart.

"That didn't hurt?"

"Like a motherfucker, but it was so fucking worth it."

I laugh but only briefly, my concern for him taking over. "You need to go and lie down."

"But I'm not finished with you yet." He pouts.

"I wasn't suggesting we'd finished, just that you need to lie down." Desire floods his face as realisation dawns, but something more serious soon dampens it down. "What? What's wrong?"

Stepping back from me, he takes my face in his hands. The look on his face has nerves racing through me, and I start to panic.

"Lauren," he breathes. "I fucking love you. Not a minute has gone by in which I haven't."

The breath I was holding comes rushing out of me. "I love you too, Ben. I always have."

Our eye contact holds, silent promises passing

between us until he ruins the moment as only he can. "I think it's time you showed me. I'm an invalid, after all." Backing up, he awkwardly pulls his shirt over his head and kicks his jeans and boxers from his legs so he's standing in front of me, gloriously naked. "You're wondering how you resisted for so long, aren't you?"

"There's still time for me to change my mind."

"No fucking chance. Now, get naked and get over here."

I've no idea what time we eventually fall asleep, but when we do, it's wrapped in each other's arms. I sleep better than I have in about six years. Giving in to my feelings for him settled something inside me that's been restless all this time. I could have continued fighting, but I would have always ended up back here, in his arms. It's where I belong.

EPILOGUE

Lauren

One Month Later...

Go to our room x

PLUCKING the post-it note from the mirror, I smile as memories assault me. Excitement has butterflies taking flight in my stomach as I run up the stairs to see what's waiting for me.

When I get to the top of the stairs, I turn the opposite way I'm used to. It's going to take a while for it to feel natural. A week after I moved back in, Jenny announced that she was moving out and in with Chris. They've still not made their relationship official; they're happy to just take things as they come and enjoy each other. I can understand that, after everything they've both been through. I'm happy for them. They deserve a happily ever after.

Pushing open the door to the master bedroom, I take in our freshly painted walls and new furniture. It's the only room of the house we've changed so far, but we've got big plans once things are stable with the business.

There's a box with a giant bow sitting in the middle of the bed with another post-it note on the top.

Wear me x

SLOWLY, I pull the silk ribbon, wanting to

remember every second of this anticipation. A laugh falls from my lips when I pull the lid off and push the tissue paper aside. Lifting the new Johnson & Son's hoodie from the box, I place it down on the bed. Beneath is a stunning new maxi dress. It's not all that different from the one he bought me the last time he did this. That dress is still one of my favourites, and thankfully it still fits.

I have a quick shower before dressing and reapplying my make-up. Before heading out to find Ben, I rummage through my jewellery box and find the necklace he bought me, putting it back where it belongs.

I don't bother looking in any of the rooms; I already know he won't be inside. The glow from the fairy lights is obvious the second I step into the kitchen, making me even more anxious to find him than before. With the scent of the barbeque surrounding me, I walk out through the sliding doors, but I'm not prepared for what I find.

The decking area is even more beautiful than I imagined. Every single tree glows with lights and candles flicker on every surface. But the most breathtaking of all is Ben standing in the middle, dressed in a white shirt with the sleeves rolled up to his elbows and a pair of dark trousers, minus shoes. He looks incredible, and I'm once again reminded of how lucky I am that we were able to find our second chance. I still have moments where I worry about the future, but as each day passes, that fear gets less and less. Ben's not once given me a reason to worry. I've no doubt he's in this for the long haul now.

"Hey, baby," he whispers when I get closer. Stepping right up to him, I wrap my arms around his waist and hold him tight. It feels so good to be able to do this properly, knowing I'm not hurting him like I was before. His lips drop to my hair as his hands run down my back.

"Everything okay in the office?"

I laugh because he makes it sound like I've been far away at work when, in reality, I was just in what used to be the garages, making sure everything's ready for our first day in there tomorrow. "Yeah, we're all ready to go."

Tomorrow is our new start. Ben and Jenny sadly had to let a few more employees go, and we've had to do some serious negotiations with some of our merchants and sub-contractors, but things seem to be going in the right direction, and of course, saving on the extortionate rent as of now will be a huge help.

"Still glad you came back?" he asks for the millionth time. Even after moving back in, I wasn't sure I wanted my old job back, but Ben has a way of wording things, and a few days later, I found myself sitting at my old desk beside Erica once again. That's all changing with the new office, because Ben insisted that my desk be beside his. He's told me time and time again that this company isn't just his, but ours, and he wants me involved all the way. I'm terrified of missing something so huge again like I did with Dad, but I have total trust in Ben and his capabilities in running the company.

"You know I am. I want it to work as much as you do."

"Did IT get everything set up for Trey?" Although they joked about Trey starting immediately, things took a little longer in reality, so in the end they agreed on his start date being tomorrow.

"Yep, all good. Stop worrying."

"I'm not. I'm just excited to see how he fits in and how it all goes."

"Oh, I think he's going to fit in just fine."

"What's that look for?"

"Nothing. I just think he's already got a vested interest in what goes on in our office."

Ben's silent for a minute before the penny drops. "What the fuck has Erica done now?"

"Nothing you want to know about, I can assure you."

"Jesus, she's a pain in my arse."

"Aw, you love her really. Now, can we please stop talking about work?"

"Sure. Are you hungry?"

"Starved. But seeing as we're re-living the past tonight, I thought I needed to do something else before we eat."

We're laying out on the swing chair covered in a fluffy blanket and staring up at the star-filled sky after eating our way through the pile of food ben barbequed. Ben's eyes darken as memories hit him. "I can't argue with that. Six weeks ago, I really never thought this would be my future," Ben whispers beneath me.

"Me neither. I never wanted anything else though."

"Me neither, baby. This is it for us now. The beginning of forever. I want it all with you."

Turning in his arms, I reach up and press my lips to his. "Forever, baby."

Are you ready fro Erica's story…it's coming next!

ACKNOWLEDGMENTS

Wow! Writing Ben and Lauren's story has been one hell of an emotional ride. I knew it was going to be a little heavy, but I never expected quite what happened. It was meant to be one book, but only a few words in and I knew these two had a lot more to give. And it's not just them, because there are a few others I hope you'd like to discover a little more about. Yes, that's right, I have plans for more. Who do you think's coming next?!

A huge thank you once again to Michelle. She read every single word of all three of these books almost the moment they fell from my fingers. You lived every second of their pain, betrayals and joy right along with them. I really don't know what I'd do without you pointing out all my stupid mistakes and loving each of my characters as much as I do.

My betas: Deanna, Helen, Lindsay, Suzanne and Tracy. You waited so patiently for this final instalment and didn't harass me too much to find out if Ben and Lauren were going to get their happily ever after. Thank you for dropping everything to read their conclusion and messaging me with your every thought along the way.

Evelyn, thank you for falling for Ben and making his and Lauren's story as good as it can be and for falling for Ben right alongside me.

Andie, a massive thank you for managing to squeeze this into your unbelievably busy schedule for proofreading for me.

I also need to thank you, my readers. Thank you for being on this journey with me, for sharing, reviewing and recommending me to your friends. I really wouldn't be here without you.

I can't let this trilogy come to an end without taking a moment to appreciate the beauty of the cover and the incredibly talented James Critchley for taking such amazing shots of a man who just screams BJ to me. His real name is George RJ and for me he represents Ben perfectly. I hope you agree.

And finally, I have to thank my husband and

daughter for supporting me through these emotional books and allowing me the time to write all the words.

So, until next time,

Tracy xo

ABOUT THE AUTHOR

Tracy Lorraine is a M/F and M/M contemporary romance author. Tracy has just turned thirty and lives in a cute Cotswold village in England with her husband, baby girl and lovable but slightly crazy dog. Having always been a bookaholic with her head stuck in her Kindle, Tracy decided to try her hand at a story idea she dreamt up and hasn't looked back since.

Be the first to find out about new releases and offers. Sign up to my newsletter here.

If you want to know what I'm up to and see teasers and snippets of what I'm working on, then you need to be in my Facebook group. Join Tracy's Angels here.

Keep up to date with Tracy's books at
www.tracylorraine.com

ALSO BY TRACY LORRAINE

Falling Series

Falling for Ryan: Part One #1

Falling for Ryan: Part Two #2

Falling for Jax #3

Falling for Daniel (An Falling Series Novella)

Falling for Ruben #4

Falling for Fin #5

Falling for Lucas #6

Falling for Caleb #7

Falling for Declan #8

Falling For Liam #9

Forbidden Series

Falling for the Forbidden

Losing the Forbidden

Fighting for the Forbidden

Ruined Series

Ruined Plans #1

Ruined by Lies #2

Ruined Promises #3

Never Forget Series

Never Forget Him #1

Never Forget Us #2

Everywhere & Nowhere #3

Chasing Series

Chasing Logan

The Cocktail Girls

His Manhattan

Her Kensington

Flirt Club

His Sorority Sweetheart

Cheeky Trifle

Santa's Naughty Elf

Resolution: Exposure

Dear All Star Player

Forever Ruined (A Ruined series spin off)

Mr. Silver

Spring Break Secret Baby

His Cherry Blossom

Something Borrowed

Her Smokin' Firefighter

SNEAK PEEK

Falling for the Forbidden is a spin off from my *Falling* series. If you've not read it then keep reading for a sneak peek at *Falling for Ryan*, my friends to lovers romance that kicks off the series.

FALLING FOR RYAN: PART ONE

Molly

Eight years ago...

"MUM, I'm going to Becky's sixteenth birthday party tonight, then sleeping at Hannah's," I remind her as I walk into the kitchen where she's sat with her head in an interior design magazine, waving her hands around—presumably trying to dry her nail varnish. I pull out a can of Coke from the fridge before continuing. "I've taken the litre bottle of vodka from the drinks cabinet, and I've got a pack of condoms...

you know, just in case." I lean back against the counter and watch for a reaction. *Any* reaction.

"Uh huh."

"I'm pretty sure some of the boys are bringing ecstasy."

"Hmm..." She hums as she turns a page and studies the room pictured.

"Didn't you only have a manicure yesterday? Why are you painting your nails already?"

Now, that gets her attention. Her head snaps up the moment the words 'nails' and 'manicure' leave my mouth. Surprise, surprise; my mother cares more about that than about alcohol, drugs, sex...and me.

"Yes, I did, but I just couldn't find a thing to wear tonight."

I doubt that's actually true, seeing as she's recently turned my eldest brother's old room into her personal wardrobe after already filling her own walk-in. "So, I went to that little boutique in town this morning and found the most perfect dress. Your dad will love it, but it didn't match the colour I chose for my nails yesterday."

"Wow, what a disaster," I mutter as I leave the room. "I'll be going out in about an hour. *Not that you really care.*" I say the last bit quieter, but I'm not sure why; when I look back, Mum is once again too engrossed in her magazine to acknowledge me.

I let out a huge breath and head back up to my room to finish packing for the party. I'm getting ready with my best friend Hannah and her twin Emma, who live next door. We've all been friends for as long as I can remember. Being twins, Hannah and Emma are really close, but Hannah and I are not far behind. The three of us do almost everything together; their parents have often joked that they have triplets, really.

I always laugh along.

Even though they know what my life is like, I don't think any of them really appreciate how much I wish that were true.

I'm just shoving my fourth outfit choice for the night into my bag when I hear my brother downstairs, greeting Mum. She instantly responds to him, which makes me laugh to myself, although it's anything but funny. One of her golden boys has come to visit. I bet if he needed something, she'd ruin that new nail varnish in an instant. God, I can't wait to get out of this hellhole I call home.

"Is Molly still here?" Daniel asks.

Her reply sounds suspiciously like, "I have no idea."

Walking to the other side of the room, I rest my hands on the windowsill and blow out a long breath as I gaze out over the countryside, trying to calm myself down. I keep telling myself not to get worked up by their actions, but sometimes it's easier said than done.

"Hey sis, I'm glad you're still here," Daniel says as he enters my room a few minutes later. My brothers are a lot older than me; I was an unplanned accident fifteen and a half years ago. Daniel is my youngest older brother and, at thirty years old, he's crazy protective of me. Steven is, too, but he now has a serious girlfriend so I'm seeing less of him these days. Daniel is my idol—always has been. He doesn't take life too seriously, does exactly as he pleases, works bloody hard, but always has fun. That's exactly what I want my life to be like, and I plan on making it so—once I get out on my own.

"Hey." I only manage one word because, as soon as I see him, I burst into tears. He pulls me into a tight hug. I hate that Mum and Dad can do this to me. Can make me feel so worthless. It makes me angry every time a tear falls for their actions. I wish I could be stronger.

"What have they done now?" Daniel asks. Both

he and Steven know how our parents treat me. Hell, I couldn't count the number of arguments I've overheard about it on both hands and feet, but nothing ever changes. I'm just grateful that I have two amazing older brothers to turn to if I need to. Plus, I have my adopted family next door, who I'm pretty sure would do just about anything for me if I needed it.

"Nothing. I'm fine," I say, pulling away from him and wiping my eyes. I look at him and see the questions in his. "No, really; I'm just being a silly, hormonal teenager."

"Hmm...whatever you say, Molls. You still going to that party tonight?" I don't believe for a second that he buys my lie, but he knows it's easier for me not to discuss it. Nothing he can say is going to make any of it better, anyway.

"Of course, why?"

"I got you something." I watch as he reaches into his coat pocket and pulls out a small bottle of vodka before handing it to me.

"What's this for?" He looks at me and quirks an eyebrow. "I know it's to drink, you fool, but why are you giving it to me?"

"Because I remember what it was like being your

age, and I didn't think anyone else would be buying you some. You deserve to act your age, Molly. Let your hair down. You work too damn hard trying to get your grades. But please be sensible. I don't want to be visiting you in the hospital or be an uncle yet. Actually..." He pauses as he reaches into his back pocket and pulls out his wallet.

My eyes widen in embarrassment. "No, no, no... I'm good, you don't need to worry about that."

I hate to admit it, but Daniel is the only one who knows what I've been up to. He let himself into my room one day while I was in my ensuite to find an open box of condoms on the bed and, being the protective brother that he is, counted them and realised two were missing. I'm hoping he doesn't want more of an explanation than that, because I really don't want to sit here and explain to my adult brother that I took myself off to the doctors a while ago and got myself on the pill—you know, just in case. Wouldn't that make Mummy and Daddy proud, to be grandparents while their daughter was still a teenager? Imagine the embarrassment.

"Okay, well, have a good time tonight, and ring me if you have any problems, yeah?"

"I promise."

I know I mentioned drugs and alcohol to my mum downstairs, but my group of friends isn't really into all that. I only said it as a way to provoke her in the hopes of getting some kind of reaction. Yes, there are plenty of kids at school who are at it every weekend, but my group actually cares about getting good grades and good jobs. The bottle of vodka Daniel just handed me will probably be it for us tonight.

"See you later then, kid," he says before kissing my forehead and leaving my room.

"THAT WAS AWESOME," Hannah squeals as the three of us stumble into the twins' bedroom sometime in the early hours of Sunday morning. Emma heads straight over to her side of the room and immediately starts replacing her party clothes with her pyjamas, while Hannah and I sit on her bed and reflect on the evening.

"So...come on, spill it...where did you go with Callum?" Hannah pleads.

"Just for a walk in the garden. I told you earlier!"

"I didn't believe you then, and I still don't now. I

saw you two getting off with each other in the corner before you disappeared."

Callum is the boy at school that every girl dreams of. He's sporty, clever, funny and, of course, seriously hot, which is exactly why no one expected him to show his face tonight. But he did, and let's just say that I got to know him a little better than I did before. I'm yet to decide if that's a good thing or not.

"Will you two keep it down? I want to get up early tomorrow to do some coursework before we go to Grandma's," Emma complains from her bed.

Okay, so I said before that we work hard to get good grades, but Emma takes it to the extreme. I was actually surprised she gave herself tonight off. She's doing A-level maths already and does Spanish lessons after school to get herself an extra GCSE. I think she's putting too much pressure on herself, but she can't seem to stop in her quest to be the best accountant Oxford has ever seen.

"Sorry," we whisper simultaneously.

"So...come on, Molly, tell me," Hannah says, keeping her voice low.

I let out a frustrated breath and go for it. "Okay, so we went outside and found a quiet corner in the garden behind a bush. He pulled me down to the ground and we kissed for a while and let our hands...

roam a little." I look up at Hannah and can see her excitement about what might come next.

"Oh my God, did you have sex with him?" she asks, but says the word *sex* much quieter. I don't know why; it's only Emma who could be listening.

"No, I didn't. I sorta thought we were going to, but by the time I got into his boxers, he was so worked up that he went off like a firework!" I can't help it, I burst out laughing at the memory, earning me another grumble from Emma.

"But I thought Callum's slept with loads of girls?" Hannah asks, confused.

"That's what the rumour mill says...I would be inclined to say that this was his first experience and the rumours are just that: rumours." We fall about giggling like the schoolgirls we are; I guess that vodka hasn't totally worn off yet.

"So, you *were* going to have sex with him, then?"

"Yeah, I guess," I say, shrugging my shoulders.

"But don't you want to wait until you're in love?" she asks innocently.

The only thing I have never told my best friend is that I lost my virginity last year at a party. Hannah has a different outlook on life thanks to her normal, loving family, and I don't want to have to explain my reasons for doing what I did that night—and a few times since. I totally understand her desire to wait until she's in love, and I admire her for it, but what I needed that night—what I *still* need—is to feel wanted by someone. And that first night? That was exactly how I felt.

FALLING FOR RYAN: PART ONE

CHAPTER ONE

Molly

Present

IT'S MIDNIGHT, and I've been sat on Ryan's doorstep for nearly an hour. I've already started on one of the bottles of wine. Although it was a scorching summer's day, the heat has now worn off, the clouds have gathered, and it's lumping it down with rain. I'm trying to tuck myself into his little porch to stop from getting so wet, but with the wind direction, it's not doing much good. I'm soaked through. It was a silly idea to pick white t-shirts when

I rebranded the coffee shop; thank God for padded bras!

By the time I'd cleaned and locked up, it was just gone ten. I love working at Cocoa's and have done so since I was sixteen. Hannah and Emma's parents own it. Susan started the business after she finished university. She came into some inheritance and, with the money, Cocoa's was born. The place was a huge part of my childhood. Hannah, Emma, and I would go there after school to do homework or just chat about boys, and it pretty much stayed that way until we finished university. We still have a booth in the back corner dedicated to us.

I will forever be grateful for Susan and her husband, Pete, whom she actually met as a customer in Cocoa's. It was love at first sight for them. Not only did they give me a job, but they took me under their wing when I was much younger.

Megan, who works in the evenings, had a phone call from her boyfriend at eight o'clock saying their little boy was really sick. I let her go home to be with him and finished up the rest of the night on my own.

Once I got in my car, all I could think about was having a nice hot bath and snuggling into bed in my tiny one-bed flat with my boyfriend, Max. We've been together on and off for the past three years, but when Hannah, whom I'd lived with above the coffee shop, decided eight months ago that she wanted her own boyfriend to move into the flat, I decided it was time I moved out and left them to it. Max had suggested I move in with him. I wasn't thrilled by the idea, to be honest, but at the time I didn't have the money to find anywhere decent to live. I hate being alone. I would have had to find someone who was renting out a room anyway, so it seemed like a sensible suggestion and a logical step in our relationship.

A week later, we all moved. Me into Max's flat, and Hannah's boyfriend into the one we'd shared for the past six years.

The ten-minute drive to our home seemed to take forever. I pulled up out the front; it was weird to be parking next to Max's car. He had worked nights the whole time I'd known him.

I dragged my body up the stairs to the third floor and let myself in. I shut the door behind me; the only light was coming from the bedroom. My heart dropped into my stomach when I heard voices and strange noises coming from down the hallway. As quietly as I could, I tiptoed towards them.

When I got to the door, I couldn't believe my eyes. Now, I knew Max was no angel, but I was under the impression that we had put the past behind us when we decided to live together and had become a monogamous couple. Yes, the past few months had been a strain, but still.

What was happening before my eyes on our bed showed me how wrong I was.

I numbly slipped back down the hallway and grabbed a couple of pairs of knickers that, luckily for me, were drying on the radiator, and left.

I tried to keep myself together as I made a pit stop at the shop on my way to Ryan's house. I didn't want to be one of those emotional women sobbing in the alcohol aisle, trying to decide which bottle would make me forget.

Once I'd paid for two bottles of my favourite wine and a crate of lager for Ryan, I made my way over to his new house. He'd only moved in two weeks ago, although it was months ago that he made the decision to buy the three-story townhouse in the new development on the outskirts of the city. It was basically a pile of bricks when he took me with him to see it for the first time, but I could see why he'd fallen in love with it. It was modern and spacious, with amazing views across fields from the back. From the front, you could see all the lights from the city in the distance. Because it was yet to be finished, it meant Ryan could choose a lot of the interior to suit his taste, and he didn't have to spend his whole summer re-decorating.

Grabbing my phone, I open up my messages to re-read the conversation I'd had with him earlier. He said he was going out tonight to celebrate the end of the school year but that he wasn't expecting to be home late. I guess that didn't really go as planned—not that he'd be expecting me to be sitting here waiting for him.

I'm starting to think I should have gone somewhere else. It's not that I don't have any other options, but out of all my friends and family, Ryan knows me the best.

What we've been through this year has made us close. I think I can safely say he's turned into my best friend somewhere in the last six months.

As I wait, images of what was happening on my bed flash though my head. I guess I should have seen it coming, really. A leopard never changes it spots, right?

Eventually, the tears come flooding out. To add to my misery, I now have black mascara streaks running down my cheeks and red puffy eyes.

Finally, I see headlights coming my way and Ryan's white Honda Civic pulling into his drive. At first, he looks shocked to see me. That changes to anger as he strides towards me.

Ryan

AS I COME TO A STOP, I can see that there's a very wet Molly huddled in my porch. She looks dreadful. I come to a very quick conclusion that it's because of her dickhead of a boyfriend. I knew it was coming; it was just a matter of when.

"Ryan," Molly sobs as I lift her tiny frame off the ground and into a hug. She shakes from both the cold and the sobs wracking her body.

Tucking her into my side, I grab her bags and let us in. On the ground floor, my townhouse has a large room with French doors looking out to the courtyard garden, and a bathroom. I thought it would make an excellent gym. The middle floor is an open-plan kitchen, living, and dining room with a small cloakroom, and the top floor has three bedrooms, one being the master with ensuite and the other a large family bathroom.

I love it.

From the moment I looked at the plans, I just knew it was going to be my little piece of heaven, and I'm still in awe that I was able to buy this place. I'll be forever grateful for the generous gift from Susan and Pete. Nothing will ever make up for what we all lost, but thanks to them, I've been able to attempt to move on with my life.

Currently, there are boxes everywhere. I haven't had much time to unpack with everything I had to do at school to end the year, but my first holiday job is to get this place sorted and looking like a home.

Anger fills my veins as I lead us up to the living room. "It's going to be okay. Let's get you warm and dry and you can tell me what the fucker did." My fists clench. I want to beat the shit out of him for treating her so badly for so long.

"How do you know he's done anything?" Molly asks in a quiet voice.

"I can read you like a book, Molly Carter. Plus, he's a massive dickhead. I think I've mentioned that before. Only Max can make you feel this bad about yourself."

"Why was I so fucking stupid? I had my doubts, everyone had their doubts, but he convinced me that it was what he wanted. I'm not really surprised, but what does shock me is how much it *hurts*."

"Come on, get your arse upstairs and in the shower. I'll find you a t-shirt to wear."

AS I ROOT through a suitcase in one of the spare bedrooms, the door to my ensuite shuts. I pull out my Oxford Brookes polo and leave it on my bed. I hope my choice will make her smile, remembering happier times.

I knock lightly on the door. "Have you got everything you need?"

There's silence for a few seconds, and I can imagine her checking out all the products in the shower, realising they're all for men. Eventually, I hear a quiet "Yes" from the other side of the door.

"Okay, I'll see you downstairs when you're done. Take your time."

I gather up her wet clothes and take them with me. They may be soaked, but I can still smell her vanilla scent on them. It makes me feel oddly warm inside. She's been my rock for the past six months. I don't know what I would have done without her.

As I put everything in the washing machine, I spot her bra poking out of the pile. "What the fuck do I do with this?" I mutter to myself. Something in me wonders if it needs some kind of special cycle in the machine, but fuck if I know. I decide to shove it all in and just put it on a cool, quick wash.

That shouldn't do it much damage, right?

DOWNLOAD NOW to continue reading

Printed in Poland
by Amazon Fulfillment
Poland Sp. z o.o., Wrocław